用英語演講，從小開始

大多數人都同意，學英文應該從兒童時期開始，但是，孩子缺乏耐心，東學一點、西學一點，模模糊糊，自己也搞不清楚學了什麼，今天學的，明天就忘記了。再加上要學會話、學文法、學 KK 音標、還要背單字，許多孩子反而因此對英文產生恐懼，對他們未來的學習造成負面的影響。

挑戰長時間的英語演講

其實，孩子的學習能力很強、記憶力又好，背東西的速度非常快，只要有正確的方法和教材，一定可以發揮極大的學習效率。「一口氣背少兒英語演講①」專門爲少兒設計，每一篇演講稿有 27 句，以三句爲一組，九句爲一段，共三段，孩子背起來沒有壓力。一般的演講稿，背了後面，就忘了前面。「一口氣背少兒英語演講①」是固定格式，可以一篇接一篇地背，不論是內容、主題，都和少兒的日常生活息息相關，能夠輕易應用到平常的對話和生活上，小朋友會越背越想背，不斷地向長時間英語演講挑戰。

書中的每篇演講稿，正常速度是兩分半鐘講完，如果能背到一分半鐘內，就能變成直覺，終生不會忘記。演講稿的內容取材自美國人日常生活會話，平易近人，只要背熟，都可以運用在實際生活當中。由於孩子們所背的每一句英文，都是正確的、優美的句子，所以，他們不管是演講或說話時，都會很有信心。

用英語演講是說英文的最高境界，背演講是學英文最好的方法。「一口氣背少兒英語演講①」的發明，是「學習出版公司」最新研發的成果，也是目前所有少兒英語教材中，獨一無二的產品。在本書出版之前，這套教材已經在幾所著名小學實際使用過，效果卓著。大部分小朋友都很有表演慾，在學校裡學了東西，回家就會秀給爸爸媽媽看，這是很棒的親子互動。同樣地，孩子們背了英語演講，回到家，每次全家吃飯前，都可以表演給大家看，必定能夠增加他們的氣質和自信心。

背演講需要有聽眾

背演講最重要的，就是要有聽眾。孩子在家裡，背給所有家人聽，一背再背，熟能生巧。小孩子舌頭靈活，只要背了幾篇演講後，說起話來就字正腔圓，發音就像美國人一樣了，不必擔心會有口音的問題。現在我們只要花一點功夫來協助他們，對他們的未來就會大有幫助。孩子們現在的一小步，就等於他們未來的一大步。

孩子剛開始背演講時，也許速度會很慢，但是會漸入佳境。背了幾篇演講稿之後，也可換換口味，改背「一口氣背會話」。如此一來，小朋友不但能用英文發表演講，也會說流利的英文，英文實力自然領先別人。只要讓孩子養成自言自語說英文的習慣，英文很快就會變成他自己的語言。

劉 毅

目錄 CONTENTS

1. My Favorite Animal

Ladies and gentlemen. It's my pleasure to be here.
I'd like to tell you about my favorite animal.

There are many nice animals in the world.
My favorite animal is the dog.
Dogs are smart, kind animals.

The first dog I saw was at a friend's house.
He was a little white puppy.
He played with me and did tricks.

After that, I loved all dogs.
Every time I hear a dog bark, I'm happy.
I like to read books about dogs, too.

favorite ('fevərɪt)	animal ('ænəml̩)
nice (naɪs)	world (wɜld)
dog (dɔg)	smart (smɑrt)
kind (kaɪnd)	white (hwaɪt)
puppy ('pʌpɪ)	play (ple)
trick (trɪk)	*every time*
bark (bɑrk)	happy ('hæpɪ)
book (bʊk)	

1

Sometimes I wish I could have a puppy.
I asked my parents, but they said no.
Soon, they might change their minds.

Until then, I help friends with their
   dogs.
I feed the neighbor's puppy sometimes.
He jumps and licks my face.

Dogs have many talents.
They can find lost people.
They can swim well.

sometimes〔'sʌm,taɪmz〕	wish〔wɪʃ〕
ask〔æsk〕	
parents〔'pɛrənts〕	might〔maɪt〕
change〔tʃendʒ〕	mind〔maɪnd〕
until〔ən'tɪl〕	friend〔frɛnd〕
feed〔fid〕	
neighbor〔'nebɚ〕	jump〔dʒʌmp〕
lick〔lɪk〕	face〔fes〕
talent〔'tælənt〕	lost〔lɔst〕
people〔'pipl̩〕	swim〔swɪm〕

1

***Dogs can also protect their families*.**

They bark when any danger comes near.

These dogs are animal heroes.

Some dogs are not nice or safe.

They make scary noises and might

  bite me.

I stay away from those dogs!

Most dogs and puppies are nice.

If I get a dog, I will love him!

I want all people to like dogs, too.

That was my story. I hope you enjoyed it.
Thank you for listening.

protect (prə'tɛkt)

danger ('dendʒɚ)

hero ('hɪro)

scary ('skɛrɪ)

bite (baɪt)

love (lʌv)

family ('fæməlɪ)

come (kʌm)

safe (sef)

noise (nɔɪz)

stay away from

want (wɑnt)

1. *My Favorite Animal*

● 演講解說

Ladies and gentlemen. It's my pleasure to be here. I'd like to tell you about my favorite animal.

各位女士、各位先生。很榮幸來到這裡。我想要跟你們說我最喜愛的動物。

There are many nice animals in the world.

世界上有許多可愛的動物。

My favorite animal is the dog.

我最喜愛的動物是狗。

Dogs are smart, kind animals.

狗是聰明而且善良的動物。

The first dog I saw was at a friend's house.

我第一次看到狗，是在朋友家裡。

He was a little white puppy.

牠是一隻小白狗。

He played with me and did tricks.

牠和我玩，還表演特技。

After that, I loved all dogs.

在那之後，我喜愛所有的狗。

Every time I hear a dog bark, I'm happy.

每次我聽到狗叫聲，我會很高興。

I like to read books about dogs, too.

我也喜歡讀關於狗的書。

** —————————————————

favorite〔'fevərɪt〕*adj.* 最喜歡的
nice〔naɪs〕*adj.* 可愛的；美好的　　animal〔'ænəml〕*n.* 動物
world〔wɜld〕*adj.* 完美的；理想的　　dog〔dɔg〕*n.* 狗
smart〔smɑrt〕*adj.* 聰明的　　kind〔kaɪnd〕*adj.* 善良的
white〔hwaɪt〕*adj.* 白色的　　puppy〔'pʌpɪ〕*n.* 小狗
play〔ple〕*v.* 玩耍　　trick〔trɪk〕*n.* 把戲
every time 每次；每當　　bark〔bɑrk〕*v.* 叫；吠
happy〔'hæpɪ〕*adj.* 高興的；開心的　　book〔buk〕*n.* 書本

1

Sometimes I wish I could have a puppy.
有時我希望可以養一隻小狗。

I asked my parents, but they said no.
我問了我的父母，但是他們說不行。

Soon, they might change their minds.
不久，他們可能會改變主意。

Until then, I help friends with their dogs.
直到那時，我會幫朋友照顧他們的狗。

I feed the neighbor's puppy sometimes.
有時我會餵鄰居的小狗。

He jumps and licks my face.
牠會跳起來舔我的臉。

Dogs have many talents.
狗有很多才能。

They can find lost people.
牠們可以找到失蹤的人。

They can swim well.
牠們很會游泳。

** ————————————————

sometimes〔'sʌm,taɪmz〕*adv.* 有時候

wish〔wɪʃ〕*v.* 希望　　ask〔æsk〕*v.* 問；要求

parents〔'pɛrənts〕*n. pl.* 父母

might〔maɪt〕*aux.* 可能　　*change one's mind* 改變主意

until〔ən'tɪl〕*prep.* 直到⋯時　　friend〔frɛnd〕*n.* 朋友

feed〔fid〕*v.* 餵　　neighbor〔'nebɚ〕*n.* 鄰居

jump〔dʒʌmp〕*v.* 跳　　lick〔lɪk〕*v.* 舔　　face〔fes〕*n.* 臉

talent〔'tælənt〕*n.* 才能　　lost〔lɔst〕*adj.* 失蹤的

people〔'pipḷ〕*n. pl.* 人　　swim〔swɪm〕*v.* 游泳

1

Dogs can also protect their
  families*.*

狗也會保護牠們的家。

They bark when any danger
  comes near.

當有危險接近時，牠們會吠
叫。

These dogs are animal heroes.

這些狗是動物英雄。

Some dogs are not nice or safe.

有些狗不可愛或並不安全。

They make scary noises and
  might bite me.

牠們會發出可怕的聲音，而且
可能會咬我。

I stay away from those dogs!

我會遠離那些狗！

Most dogs and puppies are nice.

大部分的狗都很可愛。

If I get a dog, I will love him!

如果我有一隻狗，我會很愛牠！

I want all people to like dogs,
  too.

我也希望所有的人都喜歡狗。

That was my story. I hope you
enjoyed it. Thank you for listening.

那是我的故事。我希望你們喜
歡。謝謝你們聽我的演講。

＊＊─────────────

protect〔prə'tɛkt〕v. 保護　　family〔'fæməlɪ〕n. 家庭
danger〔'dendʒɚ〕n. 危險　　***come near*** 接近
hero〔'hɪro〕n. 英雄　　safe〔sef〕adj. 安全的
scary〔'skɛrɪ〕adj. 可怕的　　noise〔nɔɪz〕n. 噪音
bite〔baɪt〕v. 咬　　***stay away from*** 遠離
get〔gɛt〕v. 得到　　love〔lʌv〕v. 愛
want〔wɑnt〕v. 希望；想要

背景說明

　　動物很可愛，牠們沒有心眼，就其本能行事。自古以來，「狗」就一直被視爲人類最好的朋友，牠們似乎最懂人類的心思。本篇演講稿，要教你如何表達出對狗的喜愛跟牠們討人歡心的地方。

1. *My favorite animal is the dog.*

favorite〔'fevərɪt〕*adj.* 最喜愛的

　　這句話的意思是「我最喜歡的動物是狗。」換句話説，就是「我最喜歡狗。」也可以説成：I like the dog best.（我最喜歡狗。）favorite 在這裡是形容詞，意思是「最喜愛的」，例如：

My *favorite* snack is ice cream.
（我最喜愛的點心是冰淇淋。）

Coke is my *favorite* drink.
（可口可樂是我最喜愛的飲料。）

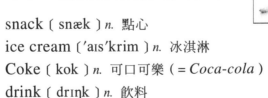

snack〔snæk〕*n.* 點心
ice cream〔'aɪs'krim〕*n.* 冰淇淋
Coke〔kok〕*n.* 可口可樂（= *Coca-cola*）
drink〔drɪŋk〕*n.* 飲料

　　另外，favorite 也可以當名詞用，做「最喜愛的人或物」解：

This book is one of my *favorites*.
（這是我最愛的書之一。）

2. *He played with me and did tricks*.

play〔ple〕*v.* 玩耍　　trick〔trɪk〕*n.* 特技；把戲
do tricks 表演特技

這句話的意思是「牠跟我玩，還表演特技。」狗除了會和人類玩，經過訓練，還會做許多特技，就是這裡說的 do tricks。常見的特技有 shake hands（握手）、sit up（坐好）、catch a ball（接球）、play dead（裝死）、beg（蹲坐舉前腳於胸前）、roll over（翻滾）等。

trick 作「特技；把戲」解時，用法如下：

My dog can do many *tricks*.
（我的狗會做很多特技。）

Magicians can perform such a *trick* as
　　pulling a rabbit out of a hat.
（魔術師會表演把兔子從帽子拉出來的這種戲法。）

magician〔mə'dʒɪʃən〕*n.* 魔術師
perform〔pɚ'fɔrm〕*v.* 表演；做
pull〔pʊl〕*v.* 拉；拖　　rabbit〔'ræbɪt〕*n.* 兔子
out of 從…之中　　hat〔hæt〕*n.* 帽子

另外，trick 也常常表示「惡作劇；花招」的意思，如果說成 play a trick on *sb*. 就是「對某人開玩笑（惡作劇）」：

John is naughty; he likes to *play tricks on*
　　his classmates.
（約翰很頑皮，他很喜歡開他同學的玩笑。）

naughty〔'nɔtɪ〕*adj.* 頑皮的
classmate〔'klæs,met〕*n.* 同班同學

1

3. ***Sometimes I wish I could have a puppy***.

sometimes〔'sʌm,taɪmz〕*adv.* 有時候

wish〔wɪʃ〕*v.* 希望　　puppy〔'pʌpɪ〕*n.* 小狗

這句話的意思是「有時候我希望  可以養一隻小狗。」這句話實際上所表示的是「我沒有養小狗」的意思。
wish 表示「希望」，必須和「假設語氣」連用，後面接名詞子句，表示「與現實相反的事實」，公式是：S + wish + (that) + S + 過去式或 were。

> I wish I were there now.
> （我真希望自己現在在那裡。）
>
> The child wishes he could go
> 　out to play.（那小孩希望他可以出去玩。）
>
> 【child〔tʃaɪld〕*n.* 小孩】

hope 則用來表示「希望會成真的事情」，例如：

> I hope everything goes well.
> （我希望一切都順利。）
>
> My mom hopes that I will enter a good
> 　college.（我母親希望我可以上好大學。）
>
> ***go well***　（進行）順利　　enter〔'ɛntɚ〕*v.* 進入
> college〔'kɑlɪdʒ〕*n.* 大學

puppy 是「小狗；幼犬」，have a puppy 的字面意思是「有一隻小狗」，就是「養一隻小狗」的意思，動詞也可以用 keep：

> I want to ***keep a dog***.（我想要養隻狗。）

1

4. **Soon, they might change their minds.**

soon〔sun〕*adv.* 不久；很快　　might〔maɪt〕*aux.* 可能
mind〔maɪnd〕*n.* 主意；想法
change *one's* **mind** 改變主意

　　這句話的意思是「不久，他們可能會改變主意。」
change *one's* mind 就是字面上「改變主意（想法）」
的意思。

　　His boss finally **changed his mind**.
（他的老闆最後改變主意。）

　　After the interview, the boss completely
　　　changed his mind about my abilities.
（面試之後，老闆對我的能力完全改觀。）

　　boss〔bɔs〕*n.* 老闆　　finally〔'faɪnḷɪ〕*adv.* 最後；終於
　　interview〔'ɪntɚ,vju〕*n.* 面試
　　completely〔kəm'plitlɪ〕*adv.* 完全地
　　ability〔ə'bɪlətɪ〕*n.* 能力

5. **They can find lost people.**

lost〔lɔst〕*adj.* 遺失的；失蹤的

　　lost 是 lose 的過去分詞，這裡是當作形容詞，
表示「遺失的；失蹤的」，lost people 意思就是「失
蹤的人」，其他像是 a lost book（不見的書）、lost
child（失蹤兒童）等，同義詞是 missing。如果說
成：I am lost. 不是指「我失蹤了。」（誤）而是：
「我迷路了。」

【missing〔'mɪsɪŋ〕*adj.* 失蹤的；找不到的】

6. *Dogs can also protect their families.*

also〔ˋɔlso〕*adv.* 也　　protect〔prəˋtɛkt〕*v.* 保護
family〔ˋfæməlɪ〕*n.* 家庭

　　這句話的意思是「狗也能保護家。」protect 是「保護」的意思，常常會和介系詞 from 連用：protect *sb.* from *sth.*，表示「保護某人免於某事」，例如：

Wearing sunglasses can *protect your eyes from the sun*.
（戴太陽眼鏡可以保護你的眼睛，免受陽光的傷害。）

A watchdog can *protect your family from danger*.（看門狗可以保護你的家人，免於危險。）

wear〔wɛr〕*v.* 戴；穿
sunglasses〔ˋsʌnˌglæsɪz〕*n. pl.* 太陽眼鏡
sun〔sʌn〕*n.* 太陽　　*the sun* 陽光
watchdog〔ˋwɑtʃˌdɔg〕*n.* 看門狗
danger〔ˋdendʒə〕*n.* 危險

這句話也可以說成：

Dogs can also defend their families.
（狗也可以保衛家。）

defend〔dɪˋfɛnd〕*v.* 保衛

　　family 的用法：當「家人」時，已經為複數；當「家庭」時，則有單數 a family 或是複數 families：

He went back to America to meet his *family*.
（他回去美國見他的家人。）

America〔əˋmɛrɪkə〕*n.* 美國　　meet〔mit〕*v.* 會見

1

7. *These dogs are animal heroes*.

hero〔ˈhɪro〕*n.* 英雄

　　這句話的意思是「這些狗是動物英雄。」因為英雄一般說來不會用來形容動物，這裡因為狗會許多才能，立下功勞，所以就成了「動物英雄」。hero 的相關詞彙有 heroine〔ˈhɛroˌɪn〕*n.* 女英雄、heroic〔hɪˈro·ɪk〕*adj.* 英勇的，要注意的是不要把女英雄拼成 heroin〔ˈhɛroˌɪn〕*n.* 海洛英，變成一種毒品就不是英雄了。

He became a national *hero* after winning the war. (贏得戰爭後，他成為了國家英雄。)

The female firefighter is a *heroine*.
(那位女消防員是女英雄。)

His *heroic* deeds have won a lot of compliments. (他的英勇事蹟贏得許多讚賞。)

national〔ˈnæʃənḷ〕*adj.* 國家的　　win〔wɪn〕*v.* 贏
war〔wɔr〕*n.* 戰爭　　female〔ˈfimel〕*adj.* 女性的
firefighter〔ˈfaɪrˌfaɪtɚ〕*n.* 消防隊員
deed〔did〕*n.* 行為
compliment〔ˈkɑmpləmənt〕*n.* 讚美

　　另外，有人默默做事，但卻未受到大家關注成為眾所皆知的英雄，可稱為「無名英雄」，英文說成：unsung hero；unsung 就是 un + sung「未受到歌頌的；被埋沒的」。

Many volunteers are *unsung heroes*.
(許多義工都是無名英雄。)

volunteer〔ˌvɑlənˈtɪr〕*n.* 義工

My Favorite Animal

1

There are many nice animals in the world. *But* my favorite animal is the dog. Dogs are smart and kind. They *also* have many talents. They can find lost people. They can swim well. They can bark at strangers and protect their families. However, some dogs are not nice. They make scary noises and might bite me. I stay away from those dogs!

I still remember the first dog I saw. It was a white puppy. He played with me and did tricks. *After that*, I loved all dogs. *Now*, every time I hear a dog bark, I am happy. I wish I could have a puppy. *But* my parents said no. *So* I play with my neighbor's dog. If I get a dog, it will be a nice dog. I will love him, and my parents will love him, too. I want all people to love dogs!

1

我最喜歡的動物

世上有許多可愛的動物。但我最喜歡的動物是狗。狗聰明而且善良。牠們也有很多才能。牠們能夠找到失蹤的人。牠們很會游泳。牠們會對陌生人吠叫,而且保護牠們的家。然而,有些狗並不可愛。牠們會發出可怕的聲音,而且可能會咬我。我會遠離那些狗。

我仍然記得我看過的第一隻狗。牠是隻白色的小狗。牠會跟我玩並表演特技。在那之後,我喜歡所有的狗。現在,每次我聽到狗叫聲,我會很高興。我希望我可以養一隻小狗。但我父母親說不行。所以我跟我鄰居的狗玩。如果我有一隻狗,牠會是一隻可愛的狗。我會愛牠,而我的父母也會愛牠。我要所有的人都喜歡狗!

2. My Favorite Story

2

Greetings to all! Old friends and new faces alike.
If you don't mind, I'm going to tell you my favorite story.

I like to listen to stories.
Stories can be sad, happy, or scary.
My favorite one is "The Three Little Pigs."

I will tell you the story now.
A long time ago, there were three pigs.
They lived with their mother in a valley.

One day, they left home to be on their own.
The first little pig was lazy.
He did not like hard work.

favorite ('fevərɪt)

story ('storɪ)

pig (pɪg)

on one's own

hard (hɑrd)

listen to

scary ('skɛrɪ)

valley ('vælɪ)

lazy ('lezɪ)

work (wɜk)

2

Because of this, ***he did something silly***.

He built his house from straw.

The second pig was also lazy.

He built his house from thin wood.

The third pig was smart and not lazy.

He built his house with rocks.

The third pig's house was very strong.

All three pigs were happy for a while.

Then, a big bad wolf came to the

　valley.

---

because of	silly〔ˈsɪlɪ〕
built〔bɪlt〕	house〔haʊs〕
straw〔strɔ〕	second〔ˈsɛkənd〕
thin〔θɪn〕	wood〔wʊd〕
third〔θɝd〕	smart〔smɑrt〕
rock〔rɑk〕	strong〔strɔŋ〕
then〔ðɛn〕	while〔hwaɪl〕
bad〔bæd〕	wolf〔wʊlf〕

2

He blew down the first pig's house.

The pig ran to his brother's house.

The wolf blew down the second pig's house.

The pigs ran to their smart brother's house.

The wolf tried to blow down that house.

The rock house was too strong to fall!

Safe inside, they laughed at the wolf.

The wolf was angry and left the valley.

The pig brothers were very happy.

Wasn't my story entertaining? It was my pleasure to tell it. I really appreciated your attention.

blow (blo)   brother ('brʌðɚ)

fall (fɔl)   safe (sef)

too···to ~   inside ('ɪn'saɪd)

laugh (læf)   angry ('æŋgrɪ)

2. *My Favorite Story*

● 演講解說

Greetings to all! Old friends and new faces alike. If you don't mind, I'm going to tell you my favorite story.

大家好！所有老朋友和新面孔。如果你不介意，我要告訴你們我最喜歡的故事。

I like to listen to stories.
Stories can be sad, happy, or scary.
My favorite one is "The Three Little Pigs."

我喜歡聽故事。
故事可能是難過的、開心的，或是可怕的。
我最喜歡的故事是「三隻小豬」。

I will tell you the story now.
A long time ago, there were three pigs.
They lived with their mother in a valley.

我現在跟你說這個故事。
很久以前，有三隻小豬。

牠們和母親住在山谷裡。

One day, they left home to be on their own.
The first little pig was lazy.
He did not like hard work.

有一天，牠們離家獨自生活。
第一隻小豬很懶惰。
牠不喜歡辛苦的工作。

** ————————————————

favorite〔'fevərɪt〕*adj.* 最喜歡的   story〔'storɪ〕*n.* 故事
listen to 聆聽   scary〔'skɛrɪ〕*adj.* 可怕的
pig〔pɪg〕*n.* 豬   valley〔'vælɪ〕*n.* 山谷
on *one's* **own** 獨自地   lazy〔'lezɪ〕*adj.* 懶惰的
hard〔hɑrd〕*adj.* 辛苦的   work〔wɝk〕*n.* 工作

Because of this, *he did something silly*.	因此，牠做了一件愚蠢的事。
He built his house from straw.	牠用稻草蓋房子。
The second pig was also lazy.	第二隻小豬也是很懶惰。
He built his house from thin wood.	牠用細細的木頭蓋房子。
The third pig was smart and not lazy.	第三隻小豬很聰明，而且不懶惰。
He built his house with rocks.	牠用石頭建造房子。
The third pig's house was very strong.	第三隻小豬的房子很堅固。
All three pigs were happy for a while.	三隻小豬都過了一段愉快的時光。
Then, a big bad wolf came to the valley.	後來，有一隻又大又壞的狼來到了山谷。

2

** ————————————————————

because of 因為　　silly〔'sɪlɪ〕*adj.* 愚蠢的
built〔bɪlt〕*v.* 建造（build 的過去式）　　house〔haʊs〕*n.* 房子
straw〔strɔ〕*n.* 稻草　　second〔'sɛkənd〕*adj.* 第二的
thin〔θɪn〕*adj.* 薄的；細的　　wood〔wʊd〕*n.* 木頭
third〔θɝd〕*adj.* 第三的　　smart〔smɑrt〕*adj.* 聰明的
rock〔rɑk〕*n.* 石頭　　strong〔strɔŋ〕*adj.* 堅固的；強壯的
happy〔'hæpɪ〕*adj.* 高興的　　while〔hwaɪl〕*n.* 一會兒；一段時間
bad〔bæd〕*adj.* 壞的　　wolf〔wʊlf〕*n.* 狼

2

He blew down the first pig's house.	牠吹倒了第一隻小豬的房子。
The pig ran to his brother's house.	牠跑到牠弟弟的房子。
The wolf blew down the second pig's house.	狼也吹倒了第二隻小豬的房子。
The pigs ran to their smart brother's house.	牠們就跑到牠們聰明弟弟的房子。
The wolf tried to blow down that house.	狼想要吹倒那棟房子。
The rock house was too strong to fall!	石頭做的房子很堅固不會倒!
Safe inside, they laughed at the wolf.	在房子裡面很安全,牠們嘲笑著狼。
The wolf was angry and left the valley.	狼很生氣,然後就離開山谷。
The pig brothers were very happy.	豬兄弟們非常高興。
Wasn't my story entertaining? It was my pleasure to tell it. I really appreciated your attention.	我的故事不是很有趣嗎?很榮幸可以跟你們說這個故事。我真的很感謝你們注意聽。

** ——————————

blow〔blo〕*v.* 吹【三態變化為:blow-blew-blown】
blow down 吹倒   brother〔'brʌðɚ〕*n.* 兄弟
try〔traɪ〕*v.* 嘗試;想要   ***too…to~*** 太…以致於不~
fall〔fɔl〕*v.* 倒塌   safe〔sef〕*adj.* 安全的
inside〔'ɪn'saɪd〕*adv.* 在裡面   laugh〔læf〕*v.* 笑
laugh at 嘲笑   angry〔'æŋgrɪ〕*adj.* 生氣的

◎背景說明

　　「三隻小豬」是大家耳熟能詳的故事，也可說是一個寓言故事。三隻小豬牠們建造房子的方式，說明了不要因爲懶惰而忽略了安全的重要性；這故事既有娛樂性，也有教育性。

1. _I like to listen to stories_.

　　listen to 聆聽　　story〔'storɪ〕_n._ 故事

　　　　這句話的意思是「我喜歡聽故事。」要特別注意的是，listen to 是「仔細聽」的意思，是持續的動作，和 hear 不同，hear 是「聽到」，是個瞬間的動作，例如：

　　　　I like to **_listen to_** music.（我喜聽音樂。）
　　　　I **_hear_** some sounds.（我聽到一些聲音。）

　　　　story 是「故事」，故事有各式各樣更細節的分類，像是 love story（愛情故事）、ghost story（鬼故事）、fairy story（童話故事）、cover story（封面故事）等。

　　ghost〔gost〕_n._ 鬼　　fairy〔fɛrɪ〕_adj._ 仙女的；幻想的
　　cover〔'kʌvɚ〕_n._ 封面

　　　　I bought the magazine because I wanted
　　　　　　to read the **_cover story_**.
　　　　（我買這本雜誌因爲我想讀封面故事。）

　　bought〔bɔt〕_v._ 買（buy 的過去式和過去分詞）
　　magazine〔ˌmægə'zin〕_n._ 雜誌
　　want〔wɑnt〕_v._ 想要

2. *One day, they left home to be on their own.*

own〔on〕*adj.* 自己的　　*on one's own* 獨自；不靠他人

　　這句話的意思是「有一天，牠們離開家獨自生活。」
on *one's* own 的意思是「一個人；不靠他人幫忙」，在
這裡是作小豬們「離家獨立過生活」解，例如：

I have been living *on my own* for several
years.（我已經獨自生活好幾年了。）

You can't expect children to do it all *on
their own*.（你不能期待小孩要不靠他人就
做全部的事情。）

live〔lɪv〕*v.* 生活；過活
several〔'sɛvərəl〕*adj.* 好幾個
expect〔ɪk'spɛkt〕*v.* 期待
children〔'tʃɪldrən〕*n. pl.* 小孩（child 的複數）

　　另一個很像的片語是 of *one's* own，意思是「屬
於自己的」，放在名詞後面做修飾：

I want to have a room *of my own*.
（我想要有我自己的房間。）

He has a mind *of his own*.（他很有主見。）

room〔rum〕*n.* 房間　　mind〔maɪnd〕*n.* 想法；意見

own 也可以當動詞用，表示「擁有」：

The rich man *owns* many houses.
（那位有錢人擁有許多房子。）

rich〔rɪtʃ〕*adj.* 有錢的　　many〔'mɛnɪ〕*adj.* 許多的
house〔haʊs〕*n.* 房子

3. ***Because of this**, he did something silly.*

because of 因為　　silly〔'sɪlɪ〕*adj.* 愚蠢的

這句話的意思是「因此，牠做了一件愚蠢的事。」
because of 後面接「名詞」，而 because 後面接「句子」。兩者的用法要區別：

Because of the rain, I decided to stay home.
（因為下雨，所以我決定待在家。）

Because it was raining, I decided to stay
　　home.（因為在下雨，所以我決定待在家。）

rain〔ren〕*n.* 雨　*v.* 下雨
decide〔dɪ'saɪd〕*v.* 決定
stay〔ste〕*v.* 停留

另外，要特別注意，如果已經使用了 because of 或
because，就不要再寫 so 了：

Because he is lazy, so he cannot find a job.【誤】
（因為他很懶惰，所以找不到工作。）

Because he is lazy, he cannot find a job.【正】

lazy〔'lezɪ〕*adj.* 懶惰的　　find〔faɪnd〕*v.* 找到
job〔dʒɑb〕*n.* 工作

這句話要注意的還有 something silly 的順序，
遇到像 something, anything, nothing, everything
這類名詞時，形容詞要放後面：

Is there ***anything wrong***?（有什麼不對勁嗎？）

wrong〔rɔŋ〕*adj.* 錯誤的；不正常的

4. *He built his house from straw.*

build〔 bɪld 〕*v.* 建造【三態變化爲:build-built-built】
straw〔 strɔ 〕*n.* 稻草

　　這句話的意思是「牠用稻草建造房子。」這裡的 from 是表示「原料的來源」，意思是「房子的原料是用稻草」，也可以寫成:The house was built of straw.（房子是用稻草建造而成。）「be built of + 材料」，表示「用…建造而成」:

The house *was built of* stone.
（那棟房子是用石頭建造而成。）
【stone〔 ston 〕*n.* 石頭】

　　如果動詞要用 make，則要注意介系詞和材料之間的關係，「be made of + 材料」，表示「用…做成」，且「原料和成品性質相同」;「be made from + 材料」，則表示「成品的性質和形狀已改變」，例如:

Bottles *are made of* glass.【性質未變】
（瓶子是由玻璃製成。）

Bread *is made from* flour.【性質已變】
（麵包是由麵粉製成。）

bottle〔'batḷ 〕*n.* 瓶子　　glass〔 glæs 〕*n.* 玻璃
bread〔 brɛd 〕*n.* 麵包　　flour〔 flaʊr 〕*n.* 麵粉

另外，be made into，則是「被製作成…」，例如:

The novel *was made into* a movie.
（這小說被拍成電影。）

novel〔'navḷ 〕*n.* 小說　　movie〔'muvɪ 〕*n.* 電影

5. ***All three pigs were happy for a while.***
   while〔hwaɪl〕*n.* 一會兒

   　　這句話的意思是「三隻小豬過了一段愉快的時光。」
   while 在此是名詞，意思是「一段時間」。而「for + 時
   間」表示「持續…」；while 前面也可加上 short 或 long，
   來表示「一小段時間」或「很長一段時間」，例如：

   　　I will wait ***for a while***.
   　　（我會等一會兒。）

   　　Please sit ***for a short while***.
   　　（請坐一下。）

   　　I haven't seen him ***for a long while***.
   　　（我很久沒看到他了。）

   　　wait〔wet〕*v.* 等待

6. ***The rock house was too strong to fall.***
   rock〔rɑk〕*n.* 石頭　　***too…to~***　太…以致於不~
   strong〔strɔŋ〕*adj.* 堅固的　　fall〔fɔl〕*v.* 倒塌

   　　這句話的意思是「石頭蓋的房子很堅固而不會倒塌。」
   使用句型「too…to + V.」，表示「太…以致於不~」。有句
   諺語是：You're never ***too old to learn***. 字面上的意思是
   「不會太老而無法學習。」意思就是「永遠都可以學習。」
   也就是中文所說的「活到老，學到老。」例如：

   　　The boy is ***too young to go*** to school.
   　　（那男孩年紀太小，還不能上學。）

2

2

The old man is *too weak to walk* fast.

（那老先生太虛弱而走不快。）

It's *too good to be* true.

（這件事太好了，而不像是真的。）

young〔jʌŋ〕*adj.* 年幼的　　weak〔wik〕*adj.* 虛弱的
walk〔wɔk〕*v.* 走路　　fast〔fæst〕*adv.* 快速地
true〔tru〕*adj.* 真實的

7. *Safe inside, they laughed at the wolf.*

safe〔sef〕*adj.* 安全的　　inside〔'ɪn'saɪd〕*adv.* 在裡面
laugh〔læf〕*v.* 笑　　*laugh at* 嘲笑
wolf〔wʊlf〕*n.* 狼

　　　這句話的意思是「在房子裡很安全，牠們嘲笑著狼。」
原本應該寫成：Because they were safe inside, they
laughed at the wolf. 經由「省略連接詞和相同的主
詞」，而變成「分詞構句」：Being safe inside, they
laughed at the wolf. 而 Being 可以省略，所以變成
文中所看到的樣子。例如：

(Being) hungry for knowledge, they
　studied hard.

（因為他們渴求知識，所以努力用功。）

Being ill, she was absent from school.

（因為生病，所以她沒來上學。）

hungry〔'hʌŋgrɪ〕*adj.* 渴望的＜*for*＞
knowledge〔'nɑlɪdʒ〕*n.* 知識
ill〔ɪl〕*adj.* 生病的　　absent〔'æbsn̩t〕*adj.* 缺席的
be absent from school 未到校；缺課

◎ 作文範例

My Favorite Story

I like to listen to stories. They can be sad, happy, or scary. My favorite story is "The Three Little Pigs." Three pigs lived in a valley with their mother. *Then*, they left home to live on their own. They needed houses. The *first* little pig was lazy. *So* he built his house out of straw. The *second* pig was also lazy. He built his house out of wood. *But* the *third* pig was not lazy. He built his house out of rocks, and it was very strong.

One day, a wolf came to the valley. It blew down the first pig's house. That pig ran to his brother's house. *Then*, the wolf blew down the second pig's house. The two pigs ran to the third pig's house. The wolf tried to blow down the third house, *but* it was too strong. The wolf was angry and left the valley. The three pig brothers were very happy.

2

● 中文翻譯

我最喜愛的故事

我喜歡聽故事。故事可以是難過的、開心的，或是可怕的。我最喜歡的故事是「三隻小豬」。三隻小豬和牠們的母親住在山谷裡。然後，牠們離家獨自生活。牠們需要房子。第一隻小豬很懶惰。所以牠用稻草蓋房子。第二隻小豬也很懶惰。牠用木頭蓋房子。但是第三隻小豬不懶惰。牠用石頭蓋房子，而且這房子很堅固。

有一天，有一隻狼來到了山谷。牠把第一小豬的房子吹倒了。牠跑到牠弟弟的房子。然後狼吹倒了第二隻小豬的房子。這兩隻小豬跑到第三隻小豬的房子。狼試著要吹倒第三棟房子，但它太堅固了。狼很生氣，而且離開了山谷。三隻豬兄弟非常高興。

3. If I Were Superman

What a wonderful audience! I can't believe my luck. It's an honor to be here.

It doesn't matter if you're a boy or girl.
You have to agree, Superman is cool.
Everyone admires him!

I sometimes pretend to be Superman.
I think about all the things I could do.
My powers would be amazing!

I'd leap tall buildings in a single bound!
People would call me a hero!
There would be a serious side to it, though.

matter〔'mætə·〕
Superman〔'supə·,mæn〕
admire〔əd'maɪr〕
pretend〔prɪ'tɛnd〕
power〔'pauə·〕
leap〔lip〕
single〔'sɪŋgḷ〕
hero〔'hɪro〕
side〔saɪd〕

agree〔ə'gri〕
cool〔kul〕
sometimes〔'sʌm,taɪmz〕
think〔θɪŋk〕
amazing〔ə'mezɪŋ〕
building〔'bɪldɪŋ〕
bound〔baund〕
serious〔'sɪrɪəs〕
though〔ðo〕

Superman knows what a real hero is.

A real hero is responsible and giving.

That's why Superman helps people.

If I were Superman, I'd help people,
　too.

I would stop the bad guys.

I would fight crime and save lives.

Sometimes I would have breaks, maybe.

During those times, I would have fun!

Nothing would be too hard for me.

real ('riəl)
responsible (rɪ'spɑnsəbḷ)　　giving ('gɪvɪŋ)
help (hɛlp)　　　　　　　　　stop (stɑp)
bad (bæd)　　　　　　　　　　guy (gaɪ)
fight (faɪt)　　　　　　　　　crime (kraɪm)
save (sev)　　　　　　　　　　lives (laɪvz)
break (brek)　　　　　　　　　maybe ('mebɪ)
time (taɪm)　　　　　　　　　*have fun*
nothing ('nʌθɪŋ)　　　　　　　hard (hɑrd)

Sports would be no problem.
I would be so strong and fast!
In no time I could be a famous athlete.

I would fly through the sky fast!
I could travel around the world in one
   day!
I would be invited to many parties!

3

These are some of the things I would do.
It's fun to imagine being Superman.
But, I am happy being myself, too.

That's what I would do if I were Superman.
It's a pretty good plan, don't you think?
Thanks for letting me share my ideas.

---

sport (spɔrt)
strong (strɔŋ)
in no time
athlete ('æθlıt)
through (θru)
travel ('trævl̩)
invite (ın'vaıt)
fun (fʌn)
happy ('hæpı)

problem ('prɑbləm)
fast (fæst)
famous ('feməs)
fly (flaı)
sky (skaı)
world (wɜld)
party ('pɑrtı)
imagine (ı'mædʒın)
myself (maı'sɛlf)

3. *If I Were Superman*

● 演講解說

What a wonderful audience! I can't believe my luck. It's an honor to be here.	好棒的聽眾呀！我無法相信我如此幸運。很榮幸來到這裡。
It doesn't matter if you're a boy or girl. You have to agree, Superman is cool. Everyone admires him!	你是男是女並不重要。你必須同意，超人很酷。每個人都欽佩他！
I sometimes pretend to be Superman. *I* think about all the things I could do. My powers would be amazing!	我有時會假裝我是超人。我會思考所有我能做的事。我的力量將會很驚人！
I'd leap tall buildings in a single bound! People would call me a hero! There would be a serious side to it, though.	我一跳就可以跳過許多高聳的建築物！人人都叫我英雄！不過這也會有比較嚴肅的一面。

** ————————————————

matter〔ˈmætɚ〕*v.* 重要　　agree〔əˈgri〕*v.* 同意
Superman〔ˈsupɚˌmæn〕*n.* 超人　　cool〔kul〕*adj.* 酷的
admire〔ədˈmaɪr〕*v.* 欽佩　　sometimes〔ˈsʌmˌtaɪmz〕*adv.* 有時
pretend〔prɪˈtɛnd〕*v.* 假裝　　think〔θɪŋk〕*v.* 想；思索
power〔ˈpaʊɚ〕*n.* 力量　　amazing〔əˈmezɪŋ〕*adj.* 驚人的
leap〔lip〕*v.* 跳過；躍過　　building〔ˈbɪldɪŋ〕*n.* 建築物
single〔ˈsɪŋgl〕*adj.* 單一的　　bound〔baʊnd〕*n.* 跳躍
hero〔ˈhɪro〕*n.* 英雄　　serious〔ˈsɪrɪəs〕*adj.* 嚴肅的
side〔saɪd〕*n.* 方面

Superman knows what a real hero is.	超人知道何謂眞正的英雄。
A real hero is responsible and giving.	一個眞正的英雄是負責且願意付出的。
That's why Superman helps people.	那就是爲何超人要幫助人們的原因。
If I were Superman, I'd help people, too.	如果我是超人，我也會幫助人們。
I would stop the bad guys.	我會制止壞蛋。
I would fight crime and save lives.	我會打擊犯罪並拯救生命。
Sometimes I would have breaks, maybe.	有時或許我會休息一下。
During those times, I would have fun!	那時候，我會玩得痛快！
Nothing would be too hard for me.	沒有什麼事對我而言會太困難。

3

** ─────────────────

real〔ˈriəl〕*adj.* 眞正的
responsible〔rɪˈspɑnsəbl̩〕*adj.* 負責的
giving〔ˈgɪvɪŋ〕*adj.* 付出的；奉獻的
stop〔stɑp〕*v.* 制止　　bad〔bæd〕*adj.* 壞的
guy〔gaɪ〕*n.* 人；傢伙　　fight〔faɪt〕*v.* 打擊；對抗
crime〔kraɪm〕*n.* 罪；犯罪行爲
save〔sev〕*v.* 拯救　　lives〔laɪvz〕*n. pl.* 生命（life 的複數）
break〔brek〕*n.* 休息；時間　　maybe〔ˈmebɪ〕*adv.* 或許；可能
time〔taɪm〕*n.* 時刻　　***have fun*** 玩得愉快
nothing〔ˈnʌθɪŋ〕*pron.* 沒什麼事情　　hard〔hɑrd〕*adj.* 困難的

***Sports would be no problem*.**   運動不是問題。
I would be so strong and fast!   我會很強壯又迅速！
In no time I could be a famous   我馬上就會是有名的運動
    athlete.   員。

I would fly through the sky fast!   我會迅速飛過天際！
I could travel around the world in   我能夠一天環遊世界！
    one day!
I would be invited to many parties!   我會受邀去很多派對！

These are some of the things I   這是一些我會去做的事情。
    would do.
It's fun to imagine being Superman.   想像是個超人很有趣。
But, I am happy being myself, too.   但是我也很高興能做我自己。

That's what I would do if I were   如果我是超人，那就是我會做
Superman. It's a pretty good plan,   的事情。這是個很好的計畫，
don't you think? Thanks for letting   你不覺得嗎？謝謝你們讓我分
me share my ideas.   享我的想法。

** ————————————————————

sport〔spɔrt〕*n.* 運動　　problem〔'prɑbləm〕*n.* 問題
strong〔strɔŋ〕*adj.* 強壯的　　fast〔fæst〕*adj.* 快速的
in no time 立刻；馬上　　famous〔'feməs〕*adj.* 有名的
athlete〔'æθlit〕*n.* 運動員　　fly〔flaɪ〕*v.* 飛行
through〔θru〕*prep.* 穿過　　sky〔skaɪ〕*n.* 天空
travel〔'trævl̩〕*v.* 旅遊　　world〔wɜld〕*n.* 世界
invite〔ɪn'vaɪt〕*v.* 邀請　　party〔'pɑrtɪ〕*n.* 派對
fun〔fʌn〕*adj.* 有趣的　　imagine〔ɪ'mædʒɪn〕*v.* 想像
happy〔'hæpɪ〕*adj.* 高興的　　myself〔maɪ'sɛlf〕*pron.* 我自己

●背景說明

　　「超人」是家喻戶曉的英雄人物。每當社會上有壞人秘密破壞人民的安詳，他便會出動打擊壞人、阻絕犯罪來維護社會上的公平與正義。如果身爲超人，有無所不能的超能力，你會怎麼做呢？

3

1. ***It doesn't matter if you're a boy or a girl.***
   matter〔'mætɚ〕*v.* 重要

　　　　這句話的意思是「你是男是女並不重要。」這個句子有個重要的文法：這裡的 It 並非一般的代名詞，而是「虛主詞」，代替後面的「名詞子句」(if you're a boy or a girl)；而這裡的 if 也不是常用的連接詞「如果」的意思，而是「是否」，可以代換爲 whether。所以這句話也可以說成：It doesn't matter whether you're a boy or a girl. 例如：

　　　　It is doubtful if (= *whether*) he will come.
　　　　（他是否會來還無法確定。）

　　　　It doesn't make any difference to me if
　　　　　　(= *whether*) it is true.
　　　　（這是否是眞的對我來說沒有差別。）

　　　　It is uncertain if (= *whether*) he will win.
　　　　（他是否會贏還無法確定。）

　　　　doubtful〔'daʊtfəl〕*adj.* 不明確的
　　　　make a difference 有差別　　true〔tru〕*adj.* 眞的
　　　　uncertain〔ʌn'sɝtn̩〕*adj.* 不確定的　　win〔wɪn〕*v.* 贏

2. ***I think about all the things I could do***.

think〔θɪŋk〕v. 想；思索　　***think about*** 思考

　　　　這句話的意思是「我思考所有我能做的事。」這句話看似有兩個動詞 think 和 could do，但是實際上是有「關係代名詞」被省略了，原本應該寫成：I think about all the things *that* I could do. 或是 I think about all the things *which* I could do. 關係代名詞作為「受詞」時，常常會省略，例如：

I don't like the book (that / which) you bought.
（我不喜歡你買的那本書。）

This is not the bag (that / which) I lost.
（這不是我弄丟的包包。）

book〔bʊk〕n. 書　　bag〔bæg〕n. 包包

　　　　另外，本句中出現的 could 是 can 的過去式，但並非表示「過去發生的事情」，而是表示「與現在事實相反的假設」。因為說話者「並不是超人」，所以他所說的事情，都是想像虛構的，所以「要用過去式助動詞表示與現在事實相反的情況」。所以接下來的句子：My powers would be amazing. 也是一樣。假設語氣常用的助動詞是 could / would / should / might，故可用助動詞來判斷是否為假設語氣：

Without air, no one could live.
（如果沒有空氣，沒有人可以生存。）

without〔wɪˈðaʊt〕prep. 沒有　　air〔ɛr〕n. 空氣
live〔lɪv〕v. 活著；生存

3. **Superman knows what a real hero is.**

knows〔no〕*v.* 知道；了解

real〔ˈriəl〕*adj.* 眞正的　　hero〔ˈhɪro〕*n.* 英雄

這句話的意思是「超人知道何謂眞正的英雄。」這句話的 what 是用來引導「名詞子句」，做 know 的受詞。其他的疑問代名詞也可以有此作用，如 who, whose, which：

I don't know **who** she is.
（我不知道她是誰。）

Tell me **what** you want.
（告訴我你要什麼。）

We are wondering **whose** hat it is.
（我們在想這是誰的帽子。）

She asked me **which** I like best.
（她問我最喜歡哪一個。）

tell〔tɛl〕*v.* 告訴　　wonder〔ˈwʌndɚ〕*v.* 想知道

hat〔hæt〕*n.* 帽子　　ask〔æsk〕*v.* 問

要特別注意，因爲這裡所引導的子句是「名詞子句」，所以「主詞和動詞不要倒裝」，疑問句才要倒裝，例如：

I don't know who is she.【誤】

I don't know who she is.【正】
（我不知道她是誰。）

Who is she?【正】（她是誰？）

4. *That's why Superman helps people*.

help〔hɛlp〕*v.* 幫助

　　　　這句話的意思是「那就是為何超人要幫助人們的原因。」
這裡的 why 用來引導「名詞子句」，也可以說成：
That's the reason why Superman helps people. 其
他一樣作用的疑問副詞有：when, where, why, how，
例如：

　　Do you know *when* and *where* she was born?
　　（你知道她是何時何地出生的嗎？）

　　I wonder *why* she hasn't come.
　　（我想知道她為何沒來。）

　　I have no idea *how* it is done.
　　（我不知道那是如何做的。）

　　reason〔'rizn̩〕*n.* 理由

5. *If I were Superman, I'd help people, too*.

　　　　這句話的意思是「如果我是超人，我也會幫助大家。」
這句話是「假設語氣」，表示和事實相反的意
思。與「現在事實相反的假設」句型：「If + S + 過去式動
詞或 were, S + would / could / should / might + V.」，
例如：

　　If he really tried, he could win the prize.
　　（如果他真的努力去做，他會得獎。）

　　If I were you, I would give up.
　　（如果我是你，我會放棄。）

　　try〔traɪ〕*v.* 嘗試　　prize〔praɪz〕*n.* 獎　　***give up*** 放棄

6. *Sometimes, I would have breaks, maybe.*

sometimes〔'sʌm,taɪmz〕*adv.* 有時候

break〔brek〕*n.* 休息；休息時間

maybe〔'mebɪ〕*adv.* 大概；或許

　　這句話的意思是「有時或許我會休息一下。」這裡的 break 是「休息」(= *rest*) 的意思，而 have a break 或 take a break，就表示「休息一下」。例如：

We have *breaks* during classes.

（上課時，我們會有下課時間。）

I usually go shopping during my lunch *break*.

（我通常在午休時間去購物。）

We have worked eight hours without a *break*.

（我們已經工作了八小時都沒有休息。）

class〔klæs〕*n.* (一堂) 課　　usually〔'juʒʊəlɪ〕*adv.* 通常

go shopping 去購物　　*lunch break* 午休時間

work〔wɝk〕*v.* 工作　　hour〔aʊr〕*n.* 小時

without〔wɪ'ðaʊt〕*prep.* 沒有

　　另外，這裡的 maybe 是副詞，就是 perhaps (或許)，記得不要和 may be (可能是) 搞混了：

Maybe I will go with you.

（或許我會跟你一起去。）

It *may be* sunny tomorrow.

（明天可能是晴天。）

sunny〔'sʌnɪ〕*adj.* 晴朗的

7. ***In no time I could be a famous athlete.***

in no time 立刻;馬上　　**famous** 〔ˈfeməs〕 *adj.* 有名的
athlete 〔ˈæθlɪt〕 *n.* 運動員

這句話的意思是「我馬上就能變成有名的運動員。」
in no time 是片語,字面上意思是「再過沒有時間」,
就是「立刻;馬上」同義的成語有:right away, right
now, at once。

3

She fell asleep ***in no time***.
(她馬上就睡著了。)

fell 〔fɛl〕 *v.* 變成 (fall 的過去式)
asleep 〔əˈslip〕 *adj.* 睡著的　　***fall asleep*** 睡著

8. ***It's fun to imagine being Superman.***

fun 〔fʌn〕 *adj.* 有趣的　　imagine 〔ɪˈmædʒɪn〕 *v.* 想像

這句話的意思是「想像是個超人很有趣。」這裡的
It 是虛主詞,代替後面的 to imagine being Superman,
所以這句話也可以寫成:To imagine being Superman is
fun. 另外,imagine 的用法是:imagine + V-ing,例如:

I can't ***imagine*** going broke.
(我無法想像破產的情況。)

Imagine flying in the sky like a bird.
(想像一下像一隻鳥兒飛翔在天空。)

go 〔go〕 *v.* 變成　　broke 〔brok〕 *adj.* 破產的
go broke 破產　　fly 〔flaɪ〕 *v.* 飛
sky 〔skaɪ〕 *n.* 天空　　bird 〔bɝd〕 *n.* 鳥

● 作文範例

If I Were Superman

Everyone admires Superman. Superman knows what a real hero is. *Sometimes* I imagine that I'm Superman. My powers would be amazing! I would jump over buildings. I would stop bad guys. I would save lives. Everyone would call me a hero. *But* mostly I would help people. A real hero is responsible and giving. That's why Superman helps people, and it's why I want to help people, too.

In my free time, I would have a lot of fun. Nothing would be too hard for me. I would be so strong and fast. I could be a famous athlete. I could travel around the world in one day. People would invite me to many parties. It's fun to imagine being Superman. *But* I'm happy being myself, too.

3

● 中文翻譯

如果我是超人

每個人都欽佩超人。超人知道什麼叫做真正的英雄。有時候我會想像我是超人。我的力量會很驚人！我會跳過很多建築物。我會制止壞蛋。我彙整救生命。每個人都會叫我英雄。但是我大多是幫助人們。一個真正的英雄是負責且願意付出的。那就是超人為何要幫助人們的原因，而這也是為何我也想要幫助人們。

在我空閒的時候，我會玩得痛快。沒有什麼事對我而言會太困難。我會很強壯又迅速。我會是個有名的運動員。我能夠一天環遊世界。人們會邀請我去很多派對。想像是個超人很有趣。但我也很高興能做我自己。

4. An Unforgettable Trip

It's great to be here today. I'm thrilled to have this opportunity.
I'm going to tell you about an unforgettable trip.

One day, **my family took a trip**.
We went to a nearby town to go shopping.
It began as a nice, **sunny day**.

As we shopped, the sky became cloudy.
For lunch, we went to a restaurant.
We sat at our table and looked outside.

Through a window, we could see the sky.
It was filled with dark, angry clouds.
It was about to storm outside!

unforgettable〔͵ʌnfɚˈgɛtəbḷ〕
nearby〔ˈnɪr͵baɪ〕
shop〔ʃɑp〕
begin〔bɪˈgɪn〕
cloudy〔ˈklaʊdɪ〕
restaurant〔ˈrɛstərənt〕
outside〔ˈaʊtˈsaɪd〕
window〔ˈwɪndo〕
be filled with
angry〔ˈæŋgrɪ〕
be about to

take a trip
town〔taʊn〕
go shopping
sunny〔ˈsʌnɪ〕
lunch〔lʌntʃ〕
table〔ˈtebḷ〕
through〔θru〕
fill〔fɪl〕
dark〔dɑrk〕
cloud〔klaʊd〕
storm〔stɔrm〕

4

The storm started as our meal was served.

The waiter was nervous about the storm.

We heard the cooks talk about it.

Everyone was very scared.

The wind blew hard and thunder
  crashed.

We saw trees being blown over.

Garbage and dust blew past our window.

We tried to eat our lunch.

There was nothing else we could do!

---

start〔stɑrt〕   meal〔mil〕
serve〔sɝv〕   waiter〔'wetɚ〕
nervous〔'nɝvəs〕   cook〔kʊk〕
scared〔skɛrd〕   wind〔wɪnd〕
blew〔blu〕   hard〔hɑrd〕
thunder〔'θʌndɚ〕   crash〔kræʃ〕
tree〔tri〕   *blow over*
garbage〔'gɑrbɪdʒ〕   dust〔dʌst〕
blew〔blu〕   past〔pæst〕
nothing〔'nʌθɪŋ〕   else〔ɛls〕

At last the storm ended.

We left the restaurant to shop more.

The town was a mess from the storm.

In the evening, we returned home.

I couldn't forget the storm.

It was exciting and scary at the same time!

I had thought going shopping would be
  boring.

I didn't even want to go.

Instead, it became an unforgettable trip!

*What did you think of my story? I really hope
you liked it. Thank you for listening and have
a great day!*

4

---

last (læst)	***at last***
end (ɛnd)	left (lɛft)
mess (mɛs)	evening ('ivnɪŋ)
return (rɪ'tɝn)	forget (fɚ'gɛt)
exciting (ɪk'saɪtɪŋ)	scary ('skɛrɪ)
at the same time	boring ('borɪŋ)
even ('ivən)	instead (ɪn'stɛd)

4. *An Unforgettable Trip*

演講解說

It's great to be here today. I'm thrilled to have this opportunity. I'm going to tell you about an unforgettable trip.

很高興今天可以來到這裡。我很興奮可以有這個機會。我要告訴你們一趟難忘的旅行。

One day, **my family took a trip.**
We went to a nearby town to go shopping.
It began as a nice, **sunny day.**

有一天，我們全家去旅行。
我們去附近的城鎮購物。

一開始是個天氣很好、晴朗的日子。

As we shopped, the sky became cloudy.
For lunch, we went to a restaurant.
We sat at our table and looked outside.

當我們購物時，天空開始烏雲密佈。
我們去一家餐廳吃午餐。
我們坐在餐桌旁，向外面看。

Through a window, we could see the sky.
It was filled with dark, angry clouds.
It was about to storm outside.

透過窗戶，我們能夠看到天空。
天空充滿漆黑洶湧的烏雲。
外面即將要有暴風雨。

** ——————————————————

unforgettable〔ˌʌnfɚˈgɛtəbl̩〕*adj.* 難忘的　　***take a trip*** 去旅行
nearby〔ˈnɪrˌbaɪ〕*adj.* 附近的　　town〔taʊn〕*n.* 城鎮
shop〔ʃɑp〕*v.* 購物　　***go shopping*** 去購物　　begin〔bɪˈgɪn〕*v.* 開始
sunny〔ˈsʌnɪ〕*adj.* 晴朗的　　cloudy〔ˈklaʊdɪ〕*adj.* 多雲的
lunch〔lʌntʃ〕*n.* 午餐　　restaurant〔ˈrɛstərənt〕*n.* 餐廳
table〔ˈtebl̩〕*n.* 餐桌　　through〔θru〕*prep.* 透過；穿過
window〔ˈwɪndo〕*n.* 窗戶　　fill〔fɪl〕*v.* 填滿；充滿
be filled with 充滿了　　dark〔dɑrk〕*adj.* 黑暗的
angry〔ˈæŋgrɪ〕*adj.*（天氣）洶湧的；險惡的　　cloud〔klaʊd〕*n.* 雲
be about to 即將　　storm〔stɔrm〕*v.* 起風暴；下暴雨　*n.* 暴風雨

The storm started as our meal was served.	當我們的餐點送上後，就開始起了暴風雨。
The waiter was nervous about the storm.	服務生很害怕暴風雨。
We heard the cooks talk about it.	我們聽到廚師在談論此事。
Everyone was very scared.	每個人都很害怕。
The wind blew hard and thunder crashed.	風吹得很強勁，雷聲轟轟作響。
We saw trees being blown over.	我們看到樹木被吹倒。
Garbage and dust blew past our window.	垃圾和灰塵吹過我們的窗外。
We tried to eat our lunch.	我們試著繼續吃午餐。
There was nothing else we could do!	我們別無他法！

4

** ─────────────────

start〔start〕*v.* 開始
meal〔mil〕*n.* 餐點
serve〔sɝv〕*v.* 供應（飯菜）
waiter〔'wetɚ〕*n.* 服務生
nervous〔'nɝvəs〕*adj.* 緊張的；害怕的　　cook〔kuk〕*n.* 廚師
scared〔skɛrd〕*adj.* 害怕的　　wind〔wɪnd〕*n.* 風
blow〔blo〕*v.* 吹【三態變化為：blow-blew-blown】
thunder〔'θʌndɚ〕*n.* 雷；雷聲　　crash〔kræʃ〕*v.* 發出爆裂聲
tree〔tri〕*n.* 樹　　***blow over***（被風）吹倒
garbage〔'gɑrbɪdʒ〕*n.* 垃圾　　dust〔dʌst〕*n.* 灰塵
past〔pæst〕*prep.* 經過　　try〔traɪ〕*v.* 嘗試；設法
nothing〔'nʌθɪŋ〕*pron.* 沒什麼事情　　else〔ɛls〕*adj.* 其他的

4

At last the storm ended.

We left the restaurant to shop more.

The town was a mess from the
　storm.

In the evening, we returned home.

I couldn't forget the storm.

It was exciting and scary at the
　same time!

I had thought going shopping
　would be boring.

I didn't even want to go.

Instead, it became an unforgettable
　trip!

What did you think of my story?
I really hope you liked it. Thank you
for listening and have a great day!

最後暴風雨結束了。

我們離開餐廳繼續購物。

因為這場暴風雨，城鎮一片
狼籍。

傍晚，我們回到家。

我無法忘記那暴風雨。

那同時讓人興奮又害怕！

我原本覺得去購物會很無
聊。

我甚至不想去。

然而，這變成了一趟難忘的
旅遊！

你覺得我的故事如何？我真
的希望你們喜歡。謝謝你們
聽我的故事，祝你們有個美
好的一天！

—— ＊＊ ——

last〔læst〕 n. 結尾　　***at last*** 最後
end〔ɛnd〕 v. 結束　　left〔lɛft〕 v. 離開 (leave 的過去式)
mess〔mɛs〕 n. 混亂　　evening〔'ivnɪŋ〕 n. 傍晚
return〔rɪ'tɜn〕 v. 返回　　forget〔fə'gɛt〕 v. 忘記
exciting〔ɪk'saɪtɪŋ〕 adj. 令人興奮的；刺激的
scary〔'skɛrɪ〕 adj. 嚇人的　　***at the same time*** 同時
boring〔'borɪŋ〕 adj. 無聊的　　even〔'ivən〕 adv. 甚至
instead〔ɪn'stɛd〕 adv. 反而；卻

背景說明

　　外出旅遊可以增廣見聞，俗話說：「萬里路勝讀萬卷書。」本篇演講稿，要教你用英文來介紹你印象最深刻的旅遊，把你的經驗生動地告訴大家。

1. ***One day***, ***my family took a trip***.

   family〔'fæməlɪ〕*n.* 家庭；家人

   trip〔trɪp〕*n.* 旅行　　***take a trip*** 去旅行

   　　trip 是「旅行；旅遊」，常常和動詞作搭配，表示「去旅行；去旅遊」，常見說法是：take a trip 或 go on a trip：

   We ***took a trip*** to the mountains last week.

   （上週我們去山區旅遊。）

   I am planning to ***go on a trip*** to Europe.

   （我正計畫要去歐洲旅遊。）

   mountain〔'maʊntn̩〕*n.* 山

   plan〔plæn〕*v.* 計畫

   Europe〔'jʊrəp〕*n.* 歐洲

   路途時間比較長的旅遊用 journey：

   After graduation, I decided to go on a ***journey***.

   （畢業後，我決定要去一趟長途旅行。）

   graduation〔ˌgrædʒʊ'eʃən〕*n.* 畢業

   journey〔'dʒɝnɪ〕*n.*（長途）旅行

   decide〔dɪ'saɪd〕*v.* 決定

2. *We went to a nearby town to go shopping*.

nearby〔'nɪr,baɪ〕*adj.* 附近的　　town〔taʊn〕*n.* 城鎮
shop〔ʃɑp〕*v.* 購物　　***go shopping*** 去購物

　　shop 是「購物」的意思，如果單單使用作為動
詞，要注意，必須寫成 shop for *sth.* (去買東西)，意思
是 buy *sth*，例如：

> My mother usually ***shops for*** vegetables
> 　in the supermarket.
> (我母親通常去超級市場買蔬菜。)

> I have to go out to ***buy*** something.
> (我必須外出買些東西。)

usually〔'juʒʊəlɪ〕*adv.* 通常
vegetable〔'vɛdʒətəbḷ〕*n.* 蔬菜
supermarket〔'supɚ,mɑrkɪt〕*n.* 超市

　　go shopping 是「去購物」，這種 go + V-ing 的
用法很多，像是：go swimming (去游泳)、go camping
(去露營)、go golfing (去打高爾夫球)、go hunting
(去打獵)、go picnicking (去野餐) 等。

> During the summer vacation, my family
> 　***went camping***.
> (暑假時，我們全家去露營。)

swim〔swɪm〕*v.* 游泳　　camp〔kæmp〕*v.* 露營
golf〔gɑlf〕*v.* 打高爾夫球　　hunt〔hʌnt〕*v.* 打獵
picnic〔'pɪknɪk〕*v.* 野餐　　summer〔'sʌmɚ〕*n.* 夏天
vacation〔ve'keʃən〕*n.* 假期
summer vacation 暑假

3. *It began as a nice, sunny day.*

begin〔bɪˋgɪn〕*v.* 開始

nice〔naɪs〕*adj.* (天氣) 好的；宜人的

sunny〔ˋsʌnɪ〕*adj.* 晴朗的

這句話的意思是「一開始是天氣好、晴朗的日子。」這裡的 It 指的是「天氣」。形容天氣的形容詞很多，有 cold (冷的)、chilly (冷颼颼的)、hot (熱的)、sultry (悶熱的)、cloudy (多雲的)、windy (颳風的)：

In Taiwan, it is *sultry* in summer.

(在台灣，夏天很悶熱。)

A storm is coming; it is *cloudy* and *windy* outside. (暴風雨要來了；外頭多雲又颳風。)

chilly〔ˋtʃɪlɪ〕*adj.* 冷颼颼的　　sultry〔ˋsʌltrɪ〕*adj.* 悶熱的
cloudy〔ˋklaʊdɪ〕*adj.* 多雲的
windy〔ˋwɪndɪ〕*adj.* 颳風的　　storm〔stɔrm〕*n.* 暴風雨

begin as 是「以…為開始」，例如：

Many important businessmen *began as* factory workers.

(很多顯赫的商人是從工廠的工人做起的。)

Our boss *began as* a reporter.

(我們老闆一開始是當記者。)

important〔ɪmˋpɔrtn̩t〕*adj.* 重要的
businessman〔ˋbɪznɪsˌmæn〕*n.* 商人
factory〔ˋfæktərɪ〕*n.* 工廠　　boss〔bɔs〕*n.* 老闆
reporter〔rɪˋportɚ〕*n.* 記者

4

4. ***It was about to storm outside.***

be about to + V. 即將～

storm〔stɔrm〕*v.* 起風暴；下大雨
outside〔'aut'said〕*adv.* 在外面

這句話的意思是「外面即將開始有暴風雨。」這裡的 It 一樣指「天氣」；be about to + V. 是慣用句型，表示「即將～」；storm 在這句中是動詞，表示「起風暴；下大雨」。以下為 be about to + V. 的用法：

We ***are about to*** start. (我們即將出發。)

I ***was*** just ***about to*** leave when he arrived.
(當他來時，我正準備要離開。)

start〔start〕*v.* 出發；啓程
just〔dʒʌst〕*adv.* 正好　　arrive〔ə'raiv〕*v.* 到達

5. ***The wind blew hard and thunder crashed.***

blew〔blu〕*v.* (風) 吹 (blow 的過去式)
hard〔hard〕*adv.* 強大地；猛烈地
thunder〔'θʌndɚ〕*n.* 雷；雷聲
crash〔kræʃ〕*v.* 發出爆裂聲

這句話的意思是「風吹得強勁，而雷聲轟轟作響。」這句話把暴風雨來臨時，風雨交加、雷聲貫耳的情景描寫得很生動，也可以說成：

The wind was strong and thunder roared.
(風很強勁，雷聲隆隆響。)

strong〔strɔŋ〕*adj.* (風) 強大的；強勁的
roar〔ror〕*v.* 轟轟作響

暴風雨來臨時，常常伴隨的天氣景象有：wind（風）、thunder（雷）、rain〔ren〕*n.* 雨、lightning〔'laɪtnɪŋ〕*n.* 閃電等。

The storm came with ***thunder*** and ***lightning***.
（暴風雨挾帶雷聲跟閃電。）

如果想要描述比較浪漫的天氣景象，可用：breeze（微風）、drizzle（毛毛雨）、rainbow（彩虹）。

I like to walk in a ***drizzle***, with a ***breeze***
　　blowing over my face and a ***rainbow***
　　hanging in the sky.
（我喜歡在毛毛雨中散步，有微風吹撫我的臉
　　龐和彩虹高掛在天空。）

drizzle〔'drɪzl̩〕*n.* 毛毛雨　　breeze〔briz〕*n.* 微風
rainbow〔'ren,bo〕*n.* 彩虹　　hang〔hæŋ〕*v.* 懸掛

6. ***We saw trees being blown over.***

tree〔tri〕*n.* 樹
blown over 吹倒

這句話的意思是「我們看到樹木正被吹倒。」這句話的動詞是 saw（看見），因為是感官動詞，所以受詞後面可以接「現在分詞」，表示「正在發生的動作」，或是「原形動詞」表示「事實」。而在本句因為樹木是「被吹倒」的，所以後面變成 being + p.p.，表示「正在被…」。常見的感官動詞有：see（看見）、hear（聽見）、feel（感受到）、listen to（聆聽）、watch（看）。

I *saw* him *enter* the room.
（我看見他進入房間。）

I *feel* the ground *shaking*.
（我感受到地面正在搖動。）

enter〔'ɛntɚ〕*v.* 進入　　ground〔graʊnd〕*n.* 地面
shake〔ʃek〕*v.* 搖動

7. *Instead*, *it became an unforgettable trip*.

instead〔ɪn'stɛd〕*adv.* 反而；卻
unforgettable〔ˌʌnfɚ'gɛtəbl̩〕*adj.* 難忘的

這句話的意思是「然而，這成了一趟難忘的旅行。」
也可說成：

However, it became an impressive trip.
（然而，這成了令人印象深刻的旅行。）

However, the trip was hard to forget.
（然而，這趟旅行很難忘。）

however〔haʊ'ɛvɚ〕*adv.* 然而
impressive〔ɪm'prɛsɪv〕*adj.* 令人印象深刻的
hard〔hɑrd〕*adj.* 困難的　　forget〔fɚ'gɛt〕*v.* 忘記

instead 另一個常見的用法是 instead of + N /
V-ing，表示「不…而～；而不是」：

***Instead of* going out, he stayed home.**
（他沒出門，而是待在家。）

Now I can walk to school ***instead of* going by**
bus.（現在我可以走路上學，而不是坐公車。）

● 作文範例

An Unforgettable Trip

Last month, I had an unforgettable trip with my family. We went shopping in a nearby town. It was a nice, sunny day. *However*, as we shopped, the sky became cloudy. At lunchtime, we went to a restaurant. We looked out the window. The sky was full of dark, angry clouds. When the storm started, everyone was very scared. The wind blew hard and thunder crashed. Trees fell over. We were happy to be inside!

At last the storm ended. The town was a mess. Trees were lying on the ground. Garbage was everywhere. In the evening, we returned home. *But* I could not forget the storm. It was exciting and scary at the same. I used to think that shopping was boring. *But* it was an unforgettable trip!

●中文翻譯

一趟難忘的旅行

上個月，我和家人有一趟難忘的旅行。我們去附近的城鎮購物。那是個天氣很好、晴朗的日子。午餐時候，我們去一家餐廳。我們向窗戶外面看。天空充滿漆黑洶湧的烏雲。當暴風雨開始的時候，每個人都很害怕。風吹得很強勁，雷聲轟轟作響。樹木倒塌。我們很高興在室內！

最後暴風雨結束了。城鎮一片狼籍。書木倒在地面上。到處是垃圾。傍晚的時候，我們回家。但是我無法忘記那場暴風雨。那同時讓人興奮又害怕。我過去覺得購物很無聊。但這是場難忘的旅遊！

5. An Important Lesson

Friends and associates. Students and parents.
It's my honor to address you.

I learned a very important lesson once.
It was a hard lesson to learn.
I will tell you about it now.

I had a cute little dog.
He was my best friend and I loved him.
It was my job to take care of him.

Sometimes I'd get lazy about my chores.
I didn't always take good care of my dog.
I would neglect him sometimes.

important〔ɪmˈpɔrtṇt〕	lesson〔ˈlɛsṇ〕
learn〔lɝn〕	once〔wʌns〕
hard〔hɑrd〕	cute〔kjut〕
job〔dʒɑb〕	*take care of*
lazy〔ˈlezɪ〕	chores〔tʃorz〕
neglect〔nɪˈglɛkt〕	

I didn't comb his fur often, though.
He didn't get bathed enough, either.
Sometimes I wouldn't take him on
　　walks.

My dog stayed in a cage by our house.
Dad told me to always do one thing.
He told me to always lock the gate
　　of the cage.

5

The lock was hard to close sometimes.
If I was in a hurry, I didn't do it.
One day, the gate came open.

comb〔kom〕 fur〔fɝ〕
though〔ðo〕 bathe〔beð〕
enough〔ə'nʌf〕 either〔'iðɚ〕
on walks stay〔ste〕
cage〔kedʒ〕 lock〔lɑk〕
gate〔get〕 hurry〔'hɝɪ〕
in a hurry came〔kem〕
open〔'opən〕

My dog escaped and ran from his cage!

I was very scared as I searched for him.

What if something bad happened to him?

We found him, but he had a hurt leg.

We bandaged it, but he was in pain.

I felt very sad about it.

I learned that I needed to be responsible.

I need to do things the right way always.

I took good care of my dog after that!

My time here is up. I hope you enjoyed my speech. Thank you for listening.

5

escape (ə'skep)   ran (ræn)

scared (skɛrd)   search (sɜtʃ)

search for   ***what if***

happen ('hæpən)   hurt (hɜt)

leg (lɛg)   bandage ('bændɪdʒ)

pain (pen)   sad (sæd)

responsible (rɪ'spɑnsəb!)

right (raɪt)   way (we)

5. *An Important Lesson*

● 演講解說

Friends and associates. Students and parents. It's my honor to address you.	各位朋友伙伴。各位學生家長。能向大家演講是我的榮幸。
I learned a very important lesson once.	我曾學到一個非常重要的教訓。
It was a hard lesson to learn.	這是一個慘痛的教訓。
I will tell you about it now.	我現在要告訴你這個教訓。
I had a cute little dog.	我養了一隻可愛的小狗。
He was my best friend and I loved him.	牠是我最好的朋友,我很愛牠。
It was my job to take care of him.	照顧牠是我的工作。
Sometimes I'd get lazy about my chores.	有時候我會懶得做一些雜事。
I didn't always take good care of my dog.	我並沒有一直好好地照顧我的狗。
I would neglect him sometimes.	我有時會忽視牠。

**

important〔ɪm'pɔrtn̩t〕*adj.* 重要的   lesson〔'lɛsn̩〕*n.* 教訓
learn〔lɝn〕*v.* 學習   once〔wʌns〕*adv.* 曾經
hard〔hɑrd〕*adj.* 辛苦的;難受的   cute〔kjut〕*adj.* 可愛的
job〔jɑb〕*n.* 工作   ***take care of*** 照顧
lazy〔'lezɪ〕*adj.* 懶惰的   chores〔tʃorz〕*n. pl.* (家庭的)雜物
    (如洗衣、打掃、整理等)   neglect〔nɪ'glɛkt〕*v.* 忽視;忽略

I didn't comb his fur often, *though*.	然而，我不常梳牠的毛。
He didn't get bathed enough, either.	牠也沒有洗足夠的澡。
Sometimes I wouldn't take him on walks.	我時候我也不會帶牠去散步。
My dog stayed in a cage by our house.	我的狗就待在我家旁邊的籠子裡。
Dad told me to always do one thing.	爸爸告訴我一定要做一件事情。
He told me to always lock the gate of the cage.	他告訴我一定要把籠子的門鎖起來。
The lock was hard to close sometimes.	那個鎖有時很難鎖。
If I was in a hurry, I didn't do it.	如果我很匆忙，我就不會鎖。
One day, the gate came open.	有一天，籠子的門打開了。

5

** ─────────────────

comb〔kom〕*v.* 梳　　fur〔fɝ〕*n.* 毛　　though〔ðo〕*adv.* 然而
bathe〔beð〕*v.* 給…洗澡　　enough〔ə'nʌf〕*adv.* 足夠地；充分地
either〔'iðɚ〕*adv.* 也（不）　　*on walks* 散步
stay〔ste〕*v.* 停留　　cage〔kedʒ〕*n.* 籠子
lock〔lɑk〕*v. n.* 鎖　　hurry〔'hɝɪ〕*n.* 急忙
in a hurry 匆忙地　　gate〔ger〕*n.* 大門
close〔kloz〕*v.* 鎖上（= *shut*）
came〔kem〕*v.* 變得（come 的過去式）
open〔'opən〕*adj.* 開著的

My dog escaped and ran from his cage!	我的狗從牠的籠子逃跑了!
I was very scared as I searched for him.	當我到處找牠時我很害怕。
What if something bad happened to him?	萬一牠發生了什麼事情該怎麼辦?
We found him, but he had a hurt leg.	我們找到牠,但是牠的腳受傷了。
We bandaged it, but he was in pain.	我們包紮牠的傷口,但牠覺得很痛。
I felt very sad about it.	我對此感到很難過。
I learned that I needed to be responsible.	我學到了我必須負責任。
I need to do things the right way always.	我必須總是把事情做對。
I took good care of my dog after that!	在那之後我就有好好地照顧我的狗!
My time here is up. I hope you enjoyed my speech. Thank you for listening.	我的時間到了。我希望你們喜歡我的演講。謝謝你們聽我演講。

5

** ————————

escape〔ə'skep〕v. 逃跑　　ran〔ræn〕v. 跑走 (run 的過去式)
scared〔skɛrd〕adj. 害怕的　　search〔sɝtʃ〕v. 搜尋
search for 尋找　　**what if**~ 如果~該怎麼辦?
happen to 發生於　　hurt〔hɝt〕adj. 受傷的　　leg〔lɛg〕n. 腳
bandage〔'bændɪdʒ〕v. 包紮　　pain〔pen〕n. 痛
be in pain 處於痛苦狀態　　sad〔sæd〕adj. 難過的
responsible〔rɪ'spɑnsəbḷ〕adj. 負責的
take good care of 好好照顧

● 背景說明

　　俗話說:「不經一事,不長一智。」人們常常都在事情發生後,或是犯了錯,才從中學到智慧。本篇演講稿,要教你如何用英文描述自己在一次的經驗中,親身體悟到教訓。

1. *It was a hard lesson to learn*.
hard〔hɑrd〕*adj.* 辛苦的;難受的
lesson〔'lɛsn̩〕*n.* 教訓　　learn〔lɜn〕*v.* 學習

　　這句話的意思是「學到了慘痛的教訓。」lesson 常見的意思是「課程;一堂課」,但是這裡 learn a lesson 則是指「學到了教訓」;而 hard 常見的意思是「困難的;硬的」,這邊和 lesson 搭配,意思「辛苦的;難受的」,表示「得來不易的教訓」,就是付出很大代價而得來的教訓,便是「慘痛的教訓」。lesson 的用法如下:

He has *learned his lesson*.
(他已經學到了教訓。)

He is too naughty; you have to *teach him a lesson*.
(他太頑皮了,你要給他點教訓。)

A lesson learned is a lesson earned.
(【諺】不經一事,不長一智。)

naughty〔'nɔtɪ〕*adj.* 頑皮的
teach sb. a lesson 給某人教訓　　earn〔ɜn〕*v.* 獲得

2. ***I didn't always take good care of my dog.***
always〔ˋɔlwez〕*adv.* 總是
take good care of 好好照顧

　　這句話字面的意思是「我沒有總是好好照顧我的
狗。」always 是「總是」，加上 not 後，變成「沒有
總是」，是「部分否定」的概念，並非全盤否定。若
要用全部否定，可用 never，例如：

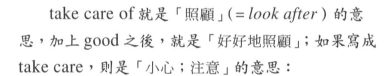

I do ***not always*** wake up early.
（我並沒有總是早起。）

I ***never*** wake up early.
（我從不早起。）

wake up 醒來；起床　　early〔ˋɜlɪ〕*adv.* 早

　　take care of 就是「照顧」（= *look after*）的意
思，加上 good 之後，就是「好好地照顧」；如果寫成
take care，則是「小心；注意」的意思：

Parents should ***take good care of*** their
　children.（父母應該好好照顧他們的小孩。）

My child is old enough to ***take care of***
　himself.
（我的小孩已夠大了，足以照顧自己。）

Take care when driving.
（開車時要小心。）

parents〔ˋpærənts〕*n. pl.* 父母
children〔ˋtʃɪldrən〕*n. pl.* 小孩（child 的複數）
drive〔draɪv〕*v.* 開車

3. *I would neglect him sometimes.*

neglect〔 nɪˈglɛkt 〕*v.* 忽視；忽略

這句話的意思是「我有時會忽視牠。」也可說成：

There were times I didn't take care of him.
（有時候我沒有照顧牠。）

On occasion I would fail to care for him.
（我有時候沒有去關心牠。）

Sometimes he did not get the attention he deserves.
（有時候牠沒有得到應得的關心。）

Every now and then I would forget to look after him.
（我有時會忘了照顧牠。）

time〔 taɪm 〕*n.* 一段時光　　*take care of* 照顧
occasion〔 əˈkeʒən 〕*n.* 時候；場合
on occasion 有時候（= *sometimes*）
fail〔 fel 〕*v.* 未能；無法　　*care for* 照顧
attention〔 əˈtɛnʃən 〕*n.* 照顧
deserve〔 dɪˈzɝv 〕*v.* 應得
every now and then 有時
look after 照顧

5

另外，照顧小狗最常做的是「餵食」，英文是 feed：

You have to *feed* your dog every day.
（你每天都必須餵你的狗。）

have to 必須　　feed〔 fid 〕*v.* 餵

4. ***I didn't comb his fur often, though.***

comb〔kom〕v. 梳　　　fur〔fɝ〕n. 毛
though〔ðo〕adv. 然而

　　　這句話的意思是「然而，我不常梳牠的毛。」
　　though 放在句末是副詞，意思是「然而」(＝ *however*)；
　句首才是常見的「連接詞」，表示「雖然」，見以下例句：

　　　Though the work was hard, I enjoyed it.
　　　（雖然這工作很困難，我去很喜歡。）

　　　The work was hard. I enjoyed it, ***though***.
　　　（這工作很困難，不過我很喜歡。）

　　　Though he is rich, he is not happy.
　　　（雖然他有錢，但他不開心。）

　　　He is rich.　He is not happy, ***though***.
　　　（他很有錢，但他不開心。）

　　　however〔hau'ɛvɚ〕adv. 然而
　　　hard〔hɑrd〕adj. 困難的
　　　enjoy〔ɪn'dʒɔɪ〕v. 喜愛　　　rich〔rɪtʃ〕adj. 有錢的

5. ***He didn't get bathed enough, either.***

bathe〔beð〕v. 給…洗澡
enough〔ə'nʌf〕adv. 足夠地　　　either〔'iðɚ〕adv. 也（不）

　　　bathe 的意思是「給…洗澡」，因為狗是「被」洗
　的，所以要用 get bathed。表示「自己洗澡」美國人
　常用 take a bath。要注意 bathe 和 bath 不同，前者
　為動詞，後者為名詞。【bath〔bæθ〕n. 洗澡】

My father helped my mother ***bathe*** the
　baby.（我爸爸幫我媽媽替嬰兒洗澡。）

I like to ***take a bath*** before sleep.
（我喜歡在睡前洗澡。）

help〔hɛlp〕*v.* 幫助　　sleep〔slip〕*n.* 睡眠；睡覺

not…either 表示「也不…」，成雙成對出現，意
思等於 neither，就是在 either 前面放個 n 就是了，
但是用法不同，neither 要放在句首形成倒裝：

You can't swim.　I can't swim, ***either***.
（你不會游泳，我也不會。）

You can't swim.　***Neither*** can I.
（你不會游泳，我也不會。）

swim〔swɪm〕*v.* 游泳

5

6. ***Sometimes I wouldn't take him on walks.***
　walk〔wɔk〕*n.* 走路；散步　　***on walks*** 散步

　　這句話的意思是「我有時不會帶牠去散步。」
on walks 或是 on a walk 就是「散步」：

You should take your dog ***on***
　a walk.
（你該帶你的狗去散步。）

I often accompany my mother ***on walks***.
（我常常陪我媽媽去散步。）

accompany〔əˈkʌmpənɪ〕*v.* 陪伴

另外,「遛狗」也可説成 walk a dog 或是 take a dog for a walk:

I *walk my dog* every morning.
(我每天早上都去遛狗。)

After dinner, my family *took our dog for a walk* in the park.
(晚餐後,我們全家去公園遛狗。)

dinner〔ˈdɪnɚ〕*n.* 晚餐　　park〔pɑrk〕*n.* 公園

5

8. *What if something bad happened to him?*
　 what if~ 如果~該怎麼辦　　*happen to* 發生於

what if~是省略句,原本寫成 what would happen if~,意思是「如果~該怎麼辦」,例如:

What if the earth stopped revolving?
= What *would happen* if the earth stopped revolving?
(如果地球停止旋轉的話,會怎麼樣?)

What if you should forget the password?
= What *would happen* if you should forget the password?
(如果萬一你忘記了密碼,該怎麼辦?)

earth〔ɝθ〕*n.* 地球　　stop〔stɑp〕*v.* 停止
revolve〔rɪˈvɑlv〕*v.* 旋轉
should〔ʃʊd〕*aux.* 萬一
forget〔fɚˈgɛt〕*v.* 忘記
password〔ˈpæsˌwɝd〕*n.* 密碼

○作文範例

An Important Lesson

I learned a very important lesson once. *At that time*, I had a cute little dog. He was my best friend and I loved him. It was my job to take care of him, *but sometimes* I was lazy. *Sometimes* I forgot to brush him, bathe him, or walk him. There was one thing that was very important. I had to lock the gate every day, or he would run away. *But* one day I forgot.

My dog ran away! I searched for him all day. *Finally*, I found him, *but* he was hurt. His leg was injured. He was in pain, and I felt very sorry. From this experience, I learned that I need to be responsible. I have to do things the right way. I took good care of my dog after that.

●中文翻譯

一個重要的教訓

　　我曾學到一個非常慘痛的教訓。在那時候,我養了一隻可愛的小狗。牠是我最好的朋友,我很愛牠。照顧牠是我的工作,但是有時候我很懶惰。我忘了要去梳牠的毛、幫牠洗澡或是帶牠去散步。有一件事情很重要。我每天必須把門鎖起來,否則牠會跑走。但是有一天我忘了。

　　我的狗逃跑了!我整天到處找牠。最後,我找到牠了,但是牠受傷了。牠的腳受傷。牠覺得很痛,而我對此感到很難過。從這個經驗中,我學到我必須負責任。我必須把事情做對。在那之後,我就有好好照顧我的狗 。

6. A Scary Experience

Ladies and gentlemen. Listeners of all ages.
You won't believe what I'm about to tell you.

Have you ever been afraid of the dark?
I was once in total darkness.
It was really a scary experience.

It happened during a typhoon.
The winds outside were blowing strongly.
The rain was coming down hard.

6

I was sitting at home with my family.
Mom called us over for dinner.
We made our way over to the kitchen.

scary (ˈskɛrɪ)　　　　experience (ɪkˈspɪrɪəns)
ever (ˈɛvɚ)　　　　　afraid (əˈfred)
be afraid of　　　　　dark (dɑrk)
once (wʌns)　　　　　total (ˈtotḷ)
darkness (ˈdɑrknɪs)　　typhoon (taɪˈfun)
wind (wɪnd)　　　　　blow (blo)
strongly (ˈstrɔŋlɪ)　　　rain (ren)
call sb. over　　　　　*make one's way to*
kitchen (ˈkɪtʃɪn,-ən)

Suddenly*, *the lights went out!

We all sat quietly for a while.

I didn't know what to do!

I couldn't see anything at all.

The television wasn't working.

My computer wouldn't turn on.

I looked outside the window.

It was completely dark outside.

There weren't any lights at all.

---

suddenly ('sʌdṇlɪ)

go out

while (hwaɪl)

television ('tɛlə͵vɪʒən)

computer (kəm'pjutɚ)

look (lʊk)

completely (kəm'plitlɪ)

light (laɪt)

quietly ('kwaɪətlɪ)

not…at all

work (wɝk)

turn on

window ('wɪndo)

I started to panic!

What if there were ghosts?

What if there were monsters?

Just then, the lights came back on.

I could see my family again.

I was so relieved!

The typhoon had caused a blackout.

It was very scary at the time.

I was glad it didn't last very long!

That was my experience. I hope it never happens again. Thank you for your attention.

6

---

panic ('pænɪk)	*what if*
ghost (gost)	monster ('mɑnstɚ)
just then	light (laɪt)
come back	on (ɑn)
family ('fæməlɪ)	relieved (rɪ'livd)
cause (kɔz)	blackout ('blæk,aʊt)
glad (glæd)	last (læst)

6. A Scary Experience

演講解說

Ladies and gentlemen. Listeners of all ages. You won't believe what I'm about to tell you.

各位女士先生。各年齡的聽眾。你們不會相信我正要告訴你們你事情。

Have you ever been afraid of the dark?
I was once in total darkness.
It was really a scary experience.

你是否害怕過黑暗？
我曾經身處漆黑。
這真是一個可怕的經驗。

It happened during a typhoon.
The winds outside were blowing
　　strongly.
The rain was coming down hard.

這發生在颱風來的時候。
外面的風吹得強勁。

雨下得很大。

I was sitting at home with my family.
Mom called us over for dinner.
We made our way over to the kitchen.

我跟我的家人坐在家裡。
媽媽叫我們過去吃晚餐。
我們就前往廚房。

** ————————————————

ever〔ˈɛvɚ〕*adv.* 曾經　　afraid〔əˈfred〕*adj.* 害怕的
be afraid of 害怕　　dark〔dɑrk〕*n.* 黑暗；暗處　*adj.* 黑暗的
once〔wʌns〕*adv.* 曾經　　total〔ˈtotḷ〕*adj.* 完全的
darkness〔ˈdɑrknɪs〕*n.* 黑暗　　scary〔ˈskɛrɪ〕*adj.* 可怕的
experience〔ɪkˈspɪrɪəns〕*n.* 經驗　　typhoon〔taɪˈfun〕*n.* 颱風
wind〔wɪnd〕*n.* 風　　blow〔blo〕*v.* 吹
strongly〔ˈstrɔŋlɪ〕*adv.* 強勁地　　rain〔ren〕*n.* 雨
come down （雨）落下　　hard〔hɑrd〕*adv.* 猛烈地
call *sb.* **over** 叫某人過來　　**make** *one's* **way to** 前往
kitchen〔ˈkɪtʃɪn, -ən〕*n.* 廚房

Suddenly**, **the lights went out!	突然間，燈熄滅了！
We all sat quietly for a while.	我們全都靜靜地坐了一會兒。
I didn't know what to do!	我不知道該怎麼辦！
I couldn't see anything at all.	我什麼東西都看不見。
The television wasn't working.	電視也不能看了。
My computer wouldn't turn on.	我的電腦也打不開。
I looked outside the window.	我往窗戶外看。
It was completely dark outside.	外面一片漆黑。
There weren't any lights at all.	完全沒有燈光。

** ——————————————————

suddenly〔'sʌdn̩lɪ〕adv. 突然地

light〔laɪt〕n. 燈

go out 熄滅　　quietly〔'kwaɪətlɪ〕adv. 安靜地

while〔hwaɪl〕n. 一會兒　　***not…at all*** 一點也不…

television〔'tɛlə͵vɪʒən〕n. 電視　　work〔wɜk〕v. 運作

computer〔kəm'pjutɚ〕n. 電腦　　***turn on*** 打開

look〔lʊk〕v. 看

outside〔aʊt'saɪd〕prep. 向…的外面　〔͵aʊt'saɪd〕adv. 在外面

window〔'wɪndo〕n. 窗戶

completely〔kəm'plitlɪ〕adv. 完全地

6

I started to panic!
What if there were ghosts?
What if there were monsters?

我開始驚慌！
如果有鬼怎麼辦？
如果有怪物怎麼辦？

Just then, the lights came back on.
I could see my family again.
I was so relieved!

就在那時，燈又亮了。
我可以再次看到我的家人。
我感到鬆了一口氣！

The typhoon had caused a
　blackout.
It was very scary at the time.
I was glad it didn't last very
　long!

颱風造成停電。

當時眞眞的很害怕。
我很高興這種情況沒有持
續很久！

*That was my experience. I hope it
never happens again. Thank you
for your attention.*

那是我的經驗。我希望這不
會再發生。謝謝你們注意
聽。

6

** ————————————————

panic〔'pænɪk〕*v.* 驚慌
what if~　如果~該怎麼辦
ghost〔gost〕*n.* 鬼　　monster〔'mɑnstɚ〕*n.* 怪物
come back 恢復　　on〔ɑn〕*adj. adv.* 開著（的）
family〔'fæməlɪ〕*n.* 家人
relieved〔rɪ'livd〕*adj.* 放心的；鬆了一口氣的
cause〔kɔz〕*v.* 造成　　blackout〔'blæk,aut〕*n.* 停電
glad〔glæd〕*adj.* 高興的　　last〔læst〕*v.* 持續

◗ 背景說明

　　從小到大，經歷過許多事情，有快樂的、難過的、難忘的、感動的，但是有沒有一個經驗讓你覺得毛骨悚然，至今仍難以忘卻的？本篇演講稿，要教你如何生動地描述一個恐怖的經驗。

1. ***Have you ever been afraid of the dark?***

ever〔'ɛvɚ〕*adv.* 曾經　　afraid〔ə'fred〕*adj.* 害怕的
be afraid of 害怕　　dark〔dɑrk〕*n.* 黑暗；暗處

　　這句話的意思是「你是否曾害怕黑暗？」這句話用「現在完成式」來表示「從過去某時到現在的經驗」。

Have you ever been to Italy?
（你是否去過義大利？）

He has told the same joke several times.
（他講過同樣的笑話好幾次了。）

Italy〔'ɪḷɪ〕*n.* 義大利　　same〔sem〕*adj.* 相同的
joke〔dʒok〕*n.* 笑話　　several〔'sɛvərəl〕*adj.* 幾個的
time〔taɪm〕*n.* 次數

　　dark 常常是形容詞，表示「黑暗的」，在這句話中是「名詞」，常以 the dark 的型態出現，意指「黑暗」；另外，in the dark 除了指「黑暗中」，也可以引申為「不知情」。

We are ***in the dark*** about what is happening.
（我們對發生的事情並不知情。）

6

2. *We made our way over to the kitchen.*

make **one's** *way to* 前往　　kitchen〔'kɪtʃɪn,-ən〕*n.* 廚房

　　這句的意思是「我們前往廚房。」make *one's* way to 是固定用法，字面的意思是「做一條路去」，就是「前往」；類似的用法有 push *one's* way（擠出去）、feel *one's* way（摸索）、fight *one's* way（自己打拼）。例如：

She *pushed her way* through the crowd.
（她從人群中擠出去。）

It was too dark in the room, so we had to
　　feel our way out.
（房間太黑了，所以我們得摸索找到出路。）

John *fought his way* to the top.
（約翰自己打拼達到顛峰。）

crowd〔kraud〕*n.* 人群　　room〔rum〕*n.* 房間
have to + *V.* 必須　　top〔tɑp〕*n.* 最高程度；頂端

　　這句話還有一個副詞 over，意思是「從一邊到另一邊」；因為作者原本「坐在某個點」，被叫去吃飯，才從坐的那個地點到廚房，因為是從「一點到另一點」，所以才會用 make *one's* way over to。類似的用法有：

Come *over* any time; you are always welcome.
（隨時都可以過來；我永遠歡迎你。）

My friend invited me *over* for dinner.
（我朋友邀請我過去吃晚餐。）

welcome〔'wɛlkəm〕*adj.* 受歡迎的

3. *Suddenly, the lights went out.*

suddenly〔'sʌdn̩lɪ〕*adv.* 突然

light〔laɪt〕*n.* 燈　　***go out*** 熄滅

　　這句話的意思是「突然間，燈就熄滅了。」light 在這裡不是指一般的「光線」，那是不可數的，這邊可數的 light，是指「一盞一盞的燈」，所以是個可數名詞，比較下列的差別：

I could hardly see anything in the poor ***light***.
（光線不足，我幾乎看不到東西。）

Don't forget to turn the ***lights*** off when you
　　go out.（出門時，別忘了關燈。）

hardly〔'hɑrdlɪ〕*adv.* 幾乎不

poor〔pʊr〕*adj.* 不足的　　***turn off*** 關掉（電源）

　　另外，go out 一般作「外出」解，在這裡是「熄滅」的意思。這個片語是用在「自己熄滅」，如果是人為關掉或打開，可以用 put / switch / turn off（關掉）、put / switch / turn on（打開）：

When the lights ***went out***, she screamed.
（當燈光熄滅時，她尖叫。）

Please ***switch off*** the lights.
（請把燈關掉。）

Mary ***switched on*** the light in the bedroom.
（瑪麗打開臥室裡的燈。）

scream〔skrim〕*v.* 尖叫　　***switch off*** 關掉

switch on 打開　　bedroom〔'bɛd͵rum〕*n.* 臥室

4. ***I didn't know what to do!***

這句話的意思是「我不知道該怎麼辦!」what to
do 是名詞片語,是由「疑問詞＋不定詞」組合而來
的,也可以寫成:what I should do,例如:

How to do it is the problem.
= How it should be done is the problem.
(如何做是個問題。)

I don't know ***where to go***.
= I don't know where I should go.
(我不知道該何去何從。)

problem〔ˈprɑbləm〕n. 問題

6

5. ***I couldn't see anything at all.***
not…at all 一點也不…

這句話的意思是「我什麼東西都看不到。」not…
at all 是常見的搭配,表示「一點也不…」,全盤的否
定,有強調的意味,例如:

They have done ***nothing at all*** to solve
the problem.
(他們沒做任何事情來解決問題。)

He did ***not*** look well ***at all***.
(他看起來一點也不健康。)

solve〔sɑlv〕v. 解決   look〔luk〕v. 看起來
well〔wɛl〕adj. 健康的

6. *What if there were ghosts?*

what if~　如果～該怎麼辦

ghost〔gost〕*n.* 鬼

what if~ 是從 what would happen if~ 省略而來，表示「如果～該怎麼辦」常用在指發生不愉快的事情：

What if this plan fails?
（如果這計畫失敗了，該怎麼辦？）

"*What if* it rains tomorrow?"
"We will have to cancel it."
（「明天下雨怎麼辦？」「那只好取消了。」）

plan〔plæn〕*n.* 計畫　　fail〔fel〕*v.* 失敗
rain〔ren〕*v.* 下雨
cancel〔'kænsl̩〕*v.* 取消

另外，what if 寫成 what-if 則是「名詞」，表示「可能發生的事情；猜測」，例如：

Life is full of *what-ifs*.
（生命充滿許多可能性。）

When I think about all of the *what-ifs* in
　my life, I feel very anxious.
（當我考慮人生的種種可能，我覺得很焦慮。）

life〔laɪf〕*n.* 生命　　*be full of* 充滿
think about 考慮
anxious〔'æŋkʃəs〕*adj.* 焦慮的

7. *Just then*, *the light came back on*.

just then 就在那時候　　*come back* 恢復
on〔ɑn〕*adj. adv.* 開著（的）

　　這句話的意思是「就在那時，燈又亮了。」come back 這裡是「恢復」的意思；come back 的其他意思有「回來；重現記憶；再度活躍起來」：

My father went away, never to *come back*.
（我父親離開，再也沒回來了。）

His name suddenly *came back* to me.
（我突然想起他的名字。）

Miniskirts have *come back* again.
（迷你裙又流行起來了。）

suddenly〔'sʌdn̩lɪ〕*adv.* 突然
miniskirt〔'mɪnɪˌskɝt〕*n.* 迷你裙

　　這句話裡面的 on 是「開著；亮著」的意思，因為燈光是恢復原本「亮」的狀態，所以有此字；相反地，如果是「關著的；切斷的」的狀態，則用 off：

The TV was *on*, but nobody was watching it.
（電視是開著的，但是沒人在看。）

Who left all the lights *on*?
（誰讓燈都亮著的？）

Make sure all the lights are *off*.
（要確認燈都關了。）

leave〔liv〕*v.* 使⋯維持某種狀態　　*make sure* 確認

○作文範例

A Scary Experience

Are you afraid of the dark? I had a very scary experience in the dark. It happened during a typhoon. I was at home with my family. The wind was blowing hard and it was raining. *Suddenly*, all of the lights went out! I didn't know what to do. I couldn't see my family. The TV didn't work. I couldn't turn the computer on. It was completely dark outside, too. There were no lights anywhere. I started to panic. I thought about ghosts and monsters. *Then*, the lights came back on. I could see my parents again. I was so relieved! The typhoon had caused a blackout. It was only an hour, *but* it seemed much longer. I never want to be alone in the dark again!

6

●中文翻譯

一個恐怖的經驗

　　你害怕黑暗嗎？我曾經個身處黑暗，這是非常可怕的經驗。我和我的家人在家裡。風吹得強勁，而且在下雨。突然間，所有的燈熄滅了！我不知道該怎麼辦。我看不見我的家人。電視也不能看了。我的電腦也打不開。外面也是一片漆黑。完全沒有燈光。我開始驚慌。我覺得會有鬼和怪物。然後，燈又亮了。我可以再次看到我的家人。我感到鬆了一口氣！颱風造成停電。這只有維持一小時，但是看似長了許多。我不想要再次身處黑暗中！

7. Going to the Night Market

What a pleasure to be here. It's great to see so many friendly faces. I'm going to tell you a little something about me.

Sometimes I go to the night market.
Usually, I go with my parents.
It is fun and exciting!

At night, the marketplace is lit up.
The lights are any color you can imagine!
It is a beautiful sight.

There are many people, and it's noisy.
Vendors shout, and loud music fills the air.
Everyone is moving and busy.

7

---

market ('markɪt)
usually ('juʒʊəlɪ)
exciting (ɪk'saɪtɪŋ)
marketplace ('markɪt,ples)
light (laɪt)
imagine (ɪ'mædʒɪn)
noisy ('nɔɪzɪ)
shout (ʃaʊt)
music ('mjuzɪk)

night market
fun (fʌn)

lit (lɪt)
color ('kʌlɚ)
sight (saɪt)
vendor ('vɛndɚ)
loud (laʊd)
fill (fɪl)

My parents take me to food stands.

I buy little snacks, and try different
  foods.

Sometimes we eat at a restaurant.

I always play at least one carnival game.

I like it when I win a prize!

I get better at the games each time I go.

Tourists go to our night market.

I often see them there, taking photos.

They come from all over the world!

7

food〔fud〕	stand〔stænd〕
food stand	snack〔snæk〕
different〔'dɪfərənt〕	restaurant〔'rɛstərənt〕
at least	carnival〔'kɑrnəvl̩〕
game〔gem〕	win〔wɪn〕
prize〔praɪz〕	better〔'bɛtɚ〕
each time	tourist〔'tʊrɪst〕
photo〔'foto〕	***take photos***
all over	world〔wɝld〕

If I find something I like, I buy it.
Last weekend I bought a shirt there.
I also buy music and toys sometimes.

My friends meet me at the night market.
We go off together to look around.
Later, we rejoin our parents to go home.

The night market is a great place to visit!
There are many fun things to do there.
You should visit it, too!

*Would you look at the time? I hope I didn't talk
too long. Thanks and I'll see you next time.*

7

---

find (faɪnd)

bought (bɔt)

toy (tɔɪ)

meet (mit)

together (təˈgɛðɚ)

later (ˈletɚ)

great (gret)

visit (ˈvɪzɪt)

weekend (ˈwikˈɛnd)

shirt (ʃɜt)

sometimes (ˈsʌmˌtaɪmz)

go off

look around

rejoin (ˌriˈdʒɔɪn)

place (ples)

7. *Going to the Night Market*

● 演講解說

What a pleasure to be here. It's great to see so many friendly faces. I'm going to tell you a little something about me.	很榮幸來到這裡。很高興看到這麼多友善的臉孔。我要告訴你們一點關於我的事情。
Sometimes I go to the night market. ***Usually, I go with my parents.*** ***It is fun and exciting!***	我有時會去逛夜市。 我通常跟我父母去。 既有趣又刺激！
At night, the marketplace is lit up. The lights are any color you can imagine! It is a beautiful sight.	晚上的時候，市集燈火通明。 燈光的顏色，你想得到的都有。 這是美麗的景觀。
There are many people, and it's noisy. Vendors shout, and loud music fills the air. Everyone is moving and busy.	人很多，也很吵鬧。 小販呼喊叫賣，空氣中充斥吵鬧的音樂。 每個人在走動且很忙碌。

7

** ————————————————

night〔naɪt〕*n.* 夜晚　market〔'mɑrkɪt〕*n.* 市場　***night market*** 夜市
usually〔'juʒʊəlɪ〕*adv.* 通常　parents〔'pɛrənts〕*n. pl.* 父母
fun〔fʌn〕*adj.* 有趣的　exciting〔ɪk'saɪtɪŋ〕*adj.* 刺激的
marketplace〔'mɑrkɪt͵ples〕*n.* 市集　lit〔lɪt〕*v.* 點亮 (light 的過去分詞)
light〔laɪt〕*n.* 燈光　color〔'kʌlɚ〕*n.* 顏色
imagine〔ɪ'mædʒɪn〕*v.* 想像　beautiful〔'bjutəfəl〕*adj.* 美麗的
sight〔saɪt〕*n.* 景象　noisy〔'nɔɪzɪ〕*adj.* 吵鬧的
vendor〔'vɛndɚ〕*n.* 小販　shout〔ʃaʊt〕*v.* 叫喊
loud〔laʊd〕*adj.* 大聲的　music〔'mjuzɪk〕*n.* 音樂
fill〔fɪl〕*v.* 充滿　air〔ɛr〕*n.* 空氣

My parents take me to food stands.	我父母帶我到小吃攤。
I buy little snacks, and try different foods.	我買了小吃，並嚐試了不同的食物。
Sometimes we eat at a restaurant.	有時我們會在餐廳吃飯。
I always play at least one carnival game.	我總是至少會玩一個遊樂場的遊戲。
I like it when I win a prize!	當我贏得獎品的時候我會很高興！
I get better at the games each time I go.	我去每一次，就更擅長玩這些遊戲。
Tourists go to our night market.	觀光客會去我們的夜市。
I often see them there, taking photos.	我常常看到他們在那裡拍照。
They come from all over the world!	他們來自世界各地。

**

food〔fud〕*n.* 食物　　stand〔stænd〕*n.* 攤位
food stand 小吃攤　　snack〔snæk〕*n.* 小吃；點心
different〔'dɪfərənt〕*adj.* 不同的
restaurant〔'rɛstərənt〕*n.* 餐廳
at least 至少　　carnival〔'kɑrnəvl̩〕*n.* 嘉年華會；遊樂場
game〔gem〕*n.* 遊戲　　*carnival game* 娛樂遊戲
win〔wɪn〕*v.* 贏得　　prize〔praɪz〕*n.* 獎品
better〔'bɛtɚ〕*adj.* 更擅長（good 的比較級）
each time 每次　　tourist〔'tʊrɪst〕*n.* 觀光客
photo〔'foto〕*n.* 照片　　*take photos* 拍照
all over 遍及　　world〔'wɝld〕*n.* 世界

7

If I find something I like,
　I buy it.
Last weekend I bought a shirt there.
I also buy music and toys
　sometimes.

My friends meet me at the night
　market.
We go off together to look around.
Later, we rejoin our parents to go
　home.

The night market is a great place to
　visit!
There are many fun things to do
　there.
You should visit it, too!

*Would you look at the time? I hope I
didn't talk too long. Thanks and I'll
see you next time.*

如果我發現我喜歡的東西，
我就會買。
上週我在那買了一件襯衫。
我有時也買唱片和玩具。

我會和朋友在夜市見面。

我們會一起離開四處看看。
之後，我們會跟父母會合
一起回家。

夜市是個很值得去的地方！

在哪裡有很多有趣的事情可
以做。
你也應該去逛逛！

可以看一下時間嗎？我希望
我沒有講太久。謝謝你們，
再見。

** ————————————————

weekend〔'wik'ɛnd〕*n.* 週末
bought〔bɔt〕*v.* 買（buy 的過去式）
shirt〔ʃɝt〕*n.* 襯衫　　music〔'mjuzɪk〕*n.* 音樂作品
toy〔tɔɪ〕*n.* 玩具　　meet〔mit〕*v.* 和…見面　　***go off*** 離開
look around 到處看看　　later〔'letɚ〕*adv.* 後來
rejoin〔ˌri'dʒɔɪn〕*v.* 與…團聚；和…會合
great〔gret〕*adj.* 很棒的　　　place〔ples〕*n.* 地方
fun〔fʌn〕*adj.* 有趣的　　　visit〔'vɪzɪt〕*v.* 探訪；去

● 背景說明

　　台灣有許多夜市，夜市滿足我們各式各樣的需求，可以吃喝玩樂，到處看看攤位，買東西，應有盡有。本篇演講稿要用英文教你如何介紹自己去夜市的經驗，讓你可以用英文跟他人說明夜市如何多采多姿又好玩。

1. *At night, the marketplace is lit up.*

marketplace〔'mɑrkɪt͵ples〕 *n.* 市集
lit〔lɪt〕*v.* 點亮（light 的過去分詞）

　　這句話的意思是「夜晚的時候，市集燈火通明。」lit 是 light 的過去分詞，三態變化是 light-lit-lit，或是 light-lighted-lighted，意思是「點亮」，light up 便是「照亮」的意思，因為夜市本身不會自己發亮，是由許多燈光所點亮，所以用被動語態；light up 也可以用於人，表示「容光煥發；面露喜悅」。

The room *lit up*.
（房間燈亮了。）

The sky has *lighted up*.
（天空亮起來了。）

His face *lit up* when he saw his girlfriend.
（他看到女友便面露喜悅。）

sky〔skaɪ〕*n.* 天空
girlfriend〔'gɝl͵frɛnd〕*n.* 女朋友

7

2. ***Vendors shout, and loud music fills the air.***

vendor〔'vɛndɚ〕*n.* 小販　　shout〔ʃaʊt〕*v.* 叫喊
loud〔laʊd〕*adj.* 大聲的　　music〔'mjuzɪk〕*n.* 音樂
fill〔fɪl〕*v.* 充滿　　air〔ɛr〕*n.* 空氣

　　本句描寫夜市典型的情景:「小販呼喊叫賣,空氣充斥吵鬧的音樂。」本句中,小販做的動作是 shout(叫喊),當然這是爲了要招攬客人,有另一個字彙叫 peddle,用來表示「沿街叫賣;兜售」,也引申爲「散播(謠言等)」:

The old man ***peddled*** ice cream on the road.
(那老翁在路上兜售冰淇淋。)

He ***peddled*** toys from door to door.
(他挨家挨戶兜售玩具。)

She likes to ***peddle*** gossip around the town.
(她喜歡在鎮上散播謠言。)

Don't ***peddle*** lies.
(別散播謊言。)

ice cream〔'aɪs'krim〕*n.* 冰淇淋
road〔rod〕*n.* 道路　　toy〔tɔɪ〕*n.* 玩具
door〔dor〕*n.* 門;門戶　　***from door to door*** 挨家挨戶
gossip〔'gɑsəp〕*n.* 謠言　　town〔taʊn〕*n.* 城鎮
lie〔laɪ〕*n.* 謊言

　　此外,loud music fills the air 字面的意思是「吵鬧的音樂塡滿了空氣」,也就是「空氣充斥著吵鬧的音樂」。這句話也可以寫成:

The air *is filled with* loud music.

（空氣充斥著吵鬧的音樂。）

The air *is full of* loud music.

（空氣充滿著吵鬧的音樂。）

The air *is thick with* loud music.

（空氣中瀰漫著吵鬧的音樂。）

be filled with　充滿了　　full〔fʊl〕*adj.* 充滿的
be full of　充滿了　　thick〔θɪk〕*adj.* 充滿的
be thick with　充滿了

3. *I always play at least one carnival game.*

at least　至少

carnival〔ˈkɑrnəvḷ〕*n.* 嘉年華會；娛樂遊戲團

game〔gem〕*n.* 遊戲　　*carnival game*　娛樂遊戲

這句話的意思是「我總是至少會玩一個娛樂遊戲。」
這裡比較特別的是 carnival game；carnival 常見的意
思是「嘉年華會」，但是這邊不是這個意思，而是那些
「流動性的遊戲團」，如馬戲團之類，會到處巡迴表演；
而 carnival game 指的就是「流動性的娛樂遊戲」，常常
在一些如園遊會、募款會、或是遊樂園會看到，常見
的遊戲有「射飛鏢打氣球」，贏家會有獎品。在台灣
的夜市常見的除了射飛鏢，也有彈珠遊戲台等之類的。

此外，at least 是「至少」，相反是 at most（最多）。

I only spend 50 dollars *at most* on
the lunch.（我最多花 50 元吃午餐。）

7

4. **I like it when I win a prize.**

win〔wɪn〕v. 贏得
prize〔praɪz〕n. 獎品

　　這句話的意思是「當我贏得獎品，
我很開心。」like it 在這邊是「高興」的意思，
並不是指喜歡某個事物；這句話也可以寫成：

I like the feeling when I win a prize.
（我喜歡贏得獎品時的感覺。）

I feel glad when I win a prize.
（當我贏得獎品時，我會很高興。）

feeling〔ˈfilɪŋ〕n. 感覺　　glad〔glæd〕adj. 高興的

like it 表「高興」，例如：

If you don't **like it**, you may lump it.
（如果你不高興，也得容忍一下。）

He is not going to study medicine whether
　　his parents **like it** or not.
（他不打算讀醫學，不管他父母高不高興。）

I am afraid my pa won't **like it**.
（我害怕我爸爸會不高興。）

lump〔lʌmp〕v.（口語）勉強忍受
study〔ˈstʌdɪ〕v. 研讀
medicine〔ˈmɛdəsn̩〕n. 醫學
afraid〔əˈfred〕adj. 害怕的
pa〔pɑ〕n.（口語）爸爸

5. *I get better at the games each time I go*.

get〔gɛt〕*v.* 變得

better〔'bɛtɚ〕*adj.* 更擅長的（good 的比較級）

each time 每次

這句話的意思是「我每次去，就更擅長玩遊戲。」
get 在此作「變得」（= *become*）解，better at 是從
good at（擅長於）而來，意思是「比較擅長於」。例如：

You will ***get better at*** chess with more practice.
（多練習，你就會更擅長下西洋棋。）

Susan ***is good at*** math.
（蘇珊擅長數學。）

chess〔tʃɛs〕*n.* 西洋棋　　practice〔'præktɪs〕*n.* 練習
math〔mæθ〕*n.* 數學（= *mathematics*）

each time 是連接詞，意思是「每次；每當」，可
以替換成：every time, no matter when, whenever。
例如：

Each time he failed, he made up his mind
　　to try harder again.
（每次他失敗的時候，他就會下定決心下次要更努力。）

Each time I see her, I blush.
（每次我看到她，就會臉紅。）

whenever〔hwɛn'ɛvɚ〕*conj.* 每當
fail〔fel〕*v.* 失敗　　***make up*** *one's **mind*** 下定決心
hard〔hɑrd〕*adv.* 努力地
blush〔blʌʃ〕*v.*（因害羞、尷尬而）臉紅

7

6. ***They come from all over the world.***

come from 來自　　**all over** 遍及

world〔wɜld〕*n.* 世界

這句話的意思是「他們來自世界各地」。

come from 是「從…來」，就是「來自；出生於」，

後面常接家庭或是國家，例如：

They ***come from*** Germany.

（他們來自德國。）

Where do you ***come from***?

（你來自哪裡？）

John ***comes from*** a wealthy family.

（約翰生於富有的家庭。）

Germany〔'dʒɜmənɪ〕*n.* 德國
wealthy〔'wɛlθɪ〕*adj.* 富有的；富裕的
family〔'fæməlɪ〕*n.* 家庭

all over 是「遍及」的意思，同義的說法有：across,

all around, throughout，例如：

He has traveled ***all over*** the world.

（他已旅行過全世界。）

The news spread ***across*** the country.

（這消息傳遍整個國家。）

travel〔'trævḷ〕*v.* 旅行
news〔njuz〕*n.* 新聞
spread〔sprɛd〕*v.* 散播

7

● 作文範例

Going to the Night Market

I love to go to the night market. It is fun and exciting! The market is bright and crowded. It is *also* noisy. Vendors shout, *and* loud music fills the air. I go there with my parents. They buy little snacks at the food stands. I love to try new foods. *Sometimes* we eat at a restaurant. I always play a game, *and sometimes* I win! If I find something I like, I buy it. I often buy music and toys.

Sometimes I meet my friends there. We look around together. *After a while*, we find our parents and go home. Tourists *also* go to our night market. They come from all over the world. The night market is a great place to visit. You should visit it, too!

7

● 中文翻譯

逛夜市

　　我喜歡去夜市。既有趣又刺激！夜市明亮而且擁擠，也很吵鬧。小販呼喊叫賣，空氣中充斥吵鬧的音樂。我和我父母一起去。他們在小吃攤買小吃。我喜歡嘗試新的食物。有時候我們會去餐廳吃飯。我總是會玩遊戲，而且我有時候玩贏！如果我發現我喜歡的東西，我就買。我常常買唱片和玩具。

　　有時候我和朋友在那裡見面。我們一起到處看看。過一會兒，我們找到我們的父母，就回家。觀光客也會來我們的夜市。他們來自世界各地。夜市是個很值得去的地方。你也應該去逛逛！

8. How I Spend My Money

Hello everybody! I'm so glad you're here.
Can I talk about how I spend my money?

Money can be a wonderful tool.
You can use it to buy things you need.
Sometimes, money buys things you want.

I don't have much money.
When I do have it, I spend it on fun things!
My parents buy stuff that I need, after all.

I buy new computer games.
My friend and I get the same games.
That way, we can play them together!

---

money ('mʌnɪ)
tool (tul)
need (nid)
spend (spɛnd)
parents ('pɛrənts)
after all
computer (kəm'pjutɚ)
way (we)

wonderful ('wʌndɚfəl)
use (juz)
sometimes ('sʌm,taɪmz)
fun (fʌn)
stuff (stʌf)
new (nju)
game (gem)
together (tə'gɛðɚ)

***Sometimes*, *I buy action figures*.**

They are based on movie characters.

Some are modeled after game characters.

I might use my money to buy candy.

I use my money to play games
at arcades.

My friends and I have a good time!

Once, I saved my money to buy
a bicycle.

I wanted a new, fancy one.

I was excited when I finally bought it!

8

action〔'ækʃən〕	figure〔'fɪgjɚ〕
action figure	base〔bes〕
be based on	movie〔'muvɪ〕
character〔'kærɪktɚ〕	model〔'madḷ〕
be modeled after	candy〔'kændɪ〕
arcade〔ɑr'ked〕	*have a good time*
once〔wʌns〕	save〔sev〕
bicycle〔'baɪsɪkḷ〕	fancy〔'fænsɪ〕
excited〔ɪk'saɪtɪd〕	finally〔'faɪnḷɪ〕

I buy hats or shoes that I like.

Or I might buy a new schoolbag.

I want to look cool.

If there's nothing I want, I save my
   money.

I can spend it if I go to the night market.

Or I can use it to buy a gift for a friend.

Having money is nice.

Sometimes I spend it; sometimes
   I save it.

I always end up spending it on fun stuff!

Well, my time is up. Thanks for listening.
I hope you were entertained by my speech.

8

hat (hæt)	shoe (ʃu)
schoolbag ('skul,bæg)	look (lʊk)
cool (kul)	*night market*
gift (gɪft)	nice (naɪs)
always ('ɔlwez)	*end up*

8. *How I Spend My Money*

● 演講解說

Hello everybody! I'm so glad you're here. Can I talk about how I spend my money?	哈囉，大家好！很高興你們來聽我演講。我可以說說我怎麼花錢嗎？
Money can be a wonderful tool. **You can use it to buy things you need.** **Sometimes**, **money buys things you want.**	錢可以是個很棒的工具。你可以用它來買你需要的東西。有時候，錢可以買你想要的東西。
I don't have much money. When I do have it, I spend it on fun things. My parents buy stuff that I need, after all.	我沒有很多錢。當我真的有錢時，我會把錢花在有趣的事物上。我父母終究只買我需要的東西。
I buy new computer games. My friends and I get the same games. That way, we can play them together.	我會買新的電腦遊戲。我的朋友跟我買一樣的遊戲。那樣子，我們就能一起玩遊戲。

8

** ————————————

money〔'mʌnɪ〕*n.* 錢　　wonderful〔'wʌndəfəl〕*adj.* 很棒的
tool〔tul〕*n.* 工具　　use〔juz〕*v.* 使用　　need〔nid〕*v.* 需要
sometimes〔'sʌm,taɪmz〕*adv.* 有時；偶爾　　spend〔spɛnd〕*v.* 花（錢）
fun〔fʌn〕*adj.* 有趣的　　parents〔'pɛrənts〕*n. pl.* 父母
stuff〔stʌf〕*n.* 東西　　***after all*** 畢竟；終究　　new〔nju〕*adj.* 新的
computer〔kəm'pjutə〕*n.* 電腦　　game〔gem〕*n.* 遊戲
get〔gɛt〕*v.* 買　　way〔we〕*n.* 方式；樣子
that way 那樣一來　　together〔tə'gɛðə〕*adv.* 一起

Sometimes, *I buy action figures*.　　　有時候，我會買公仔。

They are based on movie　　　　它們是依據電影人物而做
　　characters.　　　　　　　　　成。

Some are modeled after game　　　有些是仿製遊戲中的人物。
　　characters.

I might use my money to buy candy.　我可能會用我的前買糖果。

I use my money to play games at　　我會用錢去遊樂場玩遊戲。
　　arcades.

My friends and I have a good time!　我朋友和我都玩得很愉快！

Once, I saved my money to buy a　　我曾經存錢要買一台腳踏
　　bicycle.　　　　　　　　　車。

I wanted a new fancy one.　　　　我想要一台又新又酷炫的。

I was excited when I finally bought　當我終於買了一台時，我
　　it.　　　　　　　　　　　很興奮。

8

** —————————————————

action〔'ækʃən〕*n.* 動作；姿態

figure〔'fɪgjɚ〕*n.* 人形　　*action figure* 人形玩偶；公仔

base〔bes〕*v.* 以…爲根據　　*be based on* 基於；依據

movie〔'muvɪ〕*n.* 電影　　character〔'kærɪktɚ〕*n.* 人物

model〔'madl̩〕*v.* 按模型製作　　*be modeled after* 仿製

candy〔'kændɪ〕*n.* 糖果　　arcade〔ɑr'ked〕*n.* 電子遊樂場

have a good time 玩得愉快　　once〔wʌns〕*adv.* 曾經

save〔sev〕*v.* 存（錢）　　bicycle〔'baɪsɪkl̩〕*n.* 腳踏車

fancy〔'fænsɪ〕*adj.* 酷炫的；昂貴的

excited〔ɪk'saɪted〕*adj.* 興奮的　　finally〔'faɪnl̩ɪ〕*adv.* 終於；最後

I buy hats or shoes that I like. | 我會買我喜歡的帽子或鞋子。
Or I might buy a new schoolbag. | 或者我可能會買新的書包。
I want to look cool. | 我想看起來很酷。

If there's nothing I want, I save my money. | 如果沒東西想買,我會把錢存起來。
I can spend it if I go to the night market. | 如果去夜市,我就可以花這些錢。
Or I can use it to buy a gift for a friend. | 或者我可以用這些錢來買禮物送朋友。

Having money is nice. | 有錢的感覺很好。
Sometimes I spend it; sometimes I save it. | 有時候我會把錢花掉,有時候我會存起來。
I always end up spending it on fun stuff. | 我最後總是會把錢花在有趣的事物上。

Well, my time is up. Thanks for listening. I hope you were entertained by my speech. | 嗯,我的時間到了。謝謝你們聽我演講。我希望你們喜歡我的演講。

** ———

hat〔hæt〕*n.* 帽子　　shoe〔ʃu〕*n.* 鞋子
schoolbag〔'skul,bæg〕*n.* 書包
look〔lʊk〕*v.* 看起來　　cool〔kul〕*adj.* 很酷的
night market 夜市　　gift〔gɪft〕*n.* 禮物
nice〔naɪs〕*adj.* 美好的　　always〔'ɔlwez〕*adv.* 總是
end up* + *V-ing 最後…

背景說明

　　金錢是生活上不可或缺的事物，可以用來讓我們的生活更美好、便利。因此，如何使用金錢來過生活是很重要的，要用得巧妙、有效率才不會因此浪費了得來不易的金錢。本篇演講稿，要介紹如何善用金錢。

1. ***When I do have it, I spend it on fun things!***
   spend〔spɛnd〕v. 花（錢）　　fun〔fʌn〕adj. 有趣的

　　這句話的意思是「當我真的有錢時，我會把錢花在有趣的事物上。」do 在這裡是加強語氣，翻譯成「真的；的確；一定」，例如：

> I ***do*** wish you would come.
> （我真的希望你會來。）
>
> They ***did*** go there.
> （他們的確去了那裡。）
>
> ***Do*** tell me the truth.
> （一定要告訴我實話。）

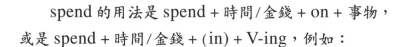

wish〔wɪʃ〕v. 希望　　truth〔truθ〕n. 實話

　　spend 的用法是 spend + 時間/金錢 + on + 事物，或是 spend + 時間/金錢 + (in) + V-ing，例如：

> I ***spend*** a lot of money ***on*** books.
> （我花很多錢買書。）

8

He *spends* too much money *on* clothes.

（他花太多錢買衣服。）

Susan *spends* a lot of time *studying*.

（蘇珊花很多時間唸書。）

My brother likes to *spend* his time *playing*
basketball.

（我弟弟喜歡花時間打籃球。）

clothes〔kloz〕*n. pl.* 衣服
study〔'stʌdɪ〕*v.* 讀書
basketball〔'bæskɪt,bɔl〕*n.* 籃球
play basketball 打籃球

2. *My parents buy stuff that I need, after all.*

stuff〔stʌf〕*n.* 東西　　need〔nid〕*v.* 需要
after all 畢竟；終究

　　stuff 是「東西」的意思，也就是 things，差別
在於 stuff 是「不可數名詞」，而 things 是「可數名詞」，
所以在使用上要特別注意各自的單複數：

Put that *stuff* over there.

（把那個東西放在那裡。）

I have to go to the supermarket
to buy some *stuff*.

（我得去超級市場買些東西。）

have to + V. 必須…
supermarket〔'supɚ,mɑrkɪt〕*n.* 超級市場

3. *That way, we can play them together*.

way〔 we 〕*n.* 方式；樣子　　*that way* 那樣一來

together〔 tə'gɛðə 〕*adv.* 一起

　　這句話的意思是「那樣一來，我們就能一起玩遊戲。」
這裡的 way 是「方式；樣子」的意思，省略了前面常
有的 in，原本寫成 in that way，表示「那樣子；以
那個方式」，例如：

I have told you not to talk *in that way*.

（我告訴過你不要那樣子講話。）

It is typical of her to act *that way*.

（那樣做是她的作風。）

It will be better *that way*.

（那樣子會比較好。）

Don't let children do things their own *way*.

（別讓孩子想怎麼做就怎麼做。）

talk〔 tɔk 〕*v.* 講話　　typical〔 'tɪpɪkḷ 〕*adj.* 典型的

be typical of sb. 是某人的特色

act〔 ækt 〕*v.* 做事　　let〔 lɛt 〕*v.* 讓

children〔 'tʃɪldrən 〕*n. pl.* 小孩（child 的複數）

8

4. *Sometimes, I buy action figures*.

action〔 'ækʃen 〕*n.* 動作；姿態

figure〔 'fɪgjə 〕*n.* 人形　　*action figure* 人形玩偶；公仔

　　action figure 字面的意思是「動作人形」，其實就
是很常見的「人形玩偶」，或在便利商店常可看到的
「公仔」。也可寫成 action doll，就是「人形娃娃」的
意思，例如：

My brother has a large collection of *action figures*.

（我弟弟收集了大量的公仔。）

Cute *action figures* are popular among teenagers.

（可愛的公仔受青少年的歡迎。）

large〔lɑrdʒ〕*adj.* 很大的
collection〔kə'lɛkʃən〕*n.* 收集
popular〔'pɑpjələ〕*adj.* 受歡迎的
among〔ə'mʌŋ〕*prep.* 在…之中
teenager〔'tin,edʒə〕*n.* 青少年

5. *They are based on movie characters.*

base〔bes〕*v.* 以…為根據
be based on 基於；根據
movie〔'muvɪ〕*n.* 電影
character〔'kærɪktə〕*n.* 角色；人物

8

　　be based on 是「基於；根據」的意思，這句話的意思是「他們是依據電影人物而做成。」其他用法的有：

The movie *is based on* a real story.
（這部電影是依據真實故事改編的。）

The report *is based on* the recent news.
（這報告是根據最近的新聞。）

real〔'riəl〕*adj.* 真實的　　report〔rɪ'port〕*n.* 報告
recent〔'risṇt〕*adj.* 最近的
news〔njuz〕*n.* 新聞

6. *Some are modeled after game characters.*
model〔'mɑdḷ〕*v.* 按模型製作
be modeled after 仿製
character〔'kærɪktɚ〕*n.* 角色；人物

　　這句話的意思是「有些是仿製遊戲角色。」some
後面省略了 action figures，因為前面已說過了；
model 名詞的意思是「模型；模特兒」，但在這裡是動
詞，意思是「按模型製作」，常以 be modeled after /
on 出現，意思為「仿製」；類似的用法有 be named
after，意思為「以…的名字命名」：

　　His haircut *is modeled after* an actor's.
　　（他的髮型是仿效一位演員。）

　　Mary *models* herself *after* her mother.
　　（瑪麗以她母親為榜樣。）

　　The fake *is modeled on* the original.
　　（這贗品是仿製原作。）

　　The baby *is named after* his father.
　　（嬰兒是以他父親的名字命名。）

　　I *name* my cat *after* a cartoon character.
　　（我依據卡通人物的名字替我的貓命名。）

　　haircut〔'hɛr,kʌt〕*n.* 髮型
　　actor〔'æktɚ〕*n.* 演員
　　cartoon〔kɑr'tun〕*n.* 卡通
　　fake〔fek〕*n.* 假貨；贗品
　　original〔ə'rɪdʒəṇl〕*n.* 原作品；原物

8

7. *I use my money to play games at arcades.*

arcade〔ɑr'ked〕*n.* 電子遊樂場

> arcade 常見的意思是「拱廊;長廊賣場」,像是 shopping arcade 便是 shopping mall(購物中心)的別稱,通常是長型的複合式商場;不過這裡的 arcade 並非指商場,而是指「電子遊樂場」,也就是有許多大型的遊樂機,投硬幣便可以使用的電子遊樂設施;也可以説成是 video arcade(美式用法),或是 amusement arcade(英式用法)。

> My children like to go to *arcades* to play games at weekends.
> (我的孩子喜歡週末去電子遊樂場打電玩。)

> *Arcades* were my favorite haunts in my childhood.
> (電子遊樂場是我兒時最愛去的地方。)

weekend〔'wik'ɛnd〕*n.* 週末
favorite〔'fevərɪt〕*adj.* 最喜歡的
haunt〔hɔnt〕*n.* 常去的地方
childhood〔'tʃaɪld,hud〕*n.* 童年時期

8

8. *I always end up spending it on fun stuff.*

end up + V-ing 最後…   fun〔fʌn〕*adj.* 有趣的

> 這句話的意思是「我總是最後會把錢花在有趣的事物上。」end up 是「結果…;最後…」,後面接「動名詞」:

> He *ended up* winning a victory.
> (他最後贏得勝利。)

win〔wɪn〕*v.* 贏得   victory〔'vɪktrɪ, vɪktərɪ〕*n.* 勝利

● 作文範例

How I Spend My Money

People spend money in different ways. You can use it to buy things you need. You can *also* use it to buy things you want. My parents buy the things I need. *So* when I have money, I spend it on fun things. I buy new computer games and action figures. *Sometimes* I buy candy, *or* I use my money to play games at arcades.

If there's nothing I want, I save my money. *Then* I can spend it on bigger things, *or* I can buy a gift for a friend. *Once* I saved so much money that I could buy a new bike! Having money is nice. *Sometimes* I spend it right away; *sometimes* I save it. *But* I always end up spending it on things I like.

8

● 中文翻譯

我如何使用金錢

人們花錢的方式不同。你可以用錢買你需要的東西。你也可以用錢來買你想要的東西。我父母買我需要的東西。所以當我有錢的時候,我把錢花在有趣的事物上。我買新的電腦遊戲和公仔。有時候我買糖果,或是我用我的錢去遊樂場玩遊戲。

如果沒有我想要的東西,我會把錢存起來。然後我可以把錢花在比較大的東西上,或是可以買禮物給我朋友。一旦我存夠多了錢,我就可以買一輛新的腳踏車!有錢很好。有時候我馬上把錢花掉;有時候我把錢存起來。但我最後都會把錢花在我喜歡的事物上。

8

9. What I Do in My Free Time

*Wow! What a great-looking crowd! Would
you like to know what I do in my free time?*

We all get breaks from time to time.
When I have free time, I rest.
I rest by doing things that I like.

One of my hobbies is drawing.
I like to draw characters from movies.
I also draw animals and comics.

Sometimes I play video games.
This is fun to do alone or with friends.
I don't play too much, though.

free ﹝ fri ﹞	*free time*
break ﹝ brek ﹞	*from time to time*
rest ﹝ rɛst ﹞	hobby ﹝ ˈhɑbɪ ﹞
draw ﹝ drɔ ﹞	character ﹝ ˈkærɪktɚ ﹞
movie ﹝ ˈmuvɪ ﹞	animal ﹝ ˈænəml̩ ﹞
comics ﹝ ˈkɑmɪks ﹞	video ﹝ ˈvɪdɪˌo ﹞
game ﹝ gem ﹞	*video game*
fun ﹝ fʌn ﹞	alone ﹝ əˈlon ﹞
friend ﹝ frɛnd ﹞	though ﹝ ðo ﹞

9

I like to talk to my friends on the Internet.
We write e-mails or chat.
We might also play online games together.

On sunny days, I play soccer and
　run fast.
When I play basketball, I try to jump high.
Playing sports with friends is fun!

On rainy days, or at night, I watch movies.
I like cartoons and action movies.
I eat popcorn and pretend I'm in a theater.

Internet〔'ɪntɚ,nɛt〕　　　e-mail〔'i,mel〕
chat〔tʃæt〕　　　　　　online〔,ɑn'laɪn〕
together〔tə'gɛðɚ〕　　　sunny〔'sʌnɪ〕
soccer〔'sɑkɚ〕　　　　　run〔rʌn〕
fast〔fæst〕　　　　　　basketball〔'bæskɪt,bɔl〕
jump〔dʒʌmp〕　　　　　high〔haɪ〕
sport〔sport〕　　　　　rainy〔'renɪ〕
night〔naɪt〕　　　　　　cartoon〔kɑr'tun〕
action〔'ækʃən〕　　　　*action movie*
popcorn〔'pɑp,kɔrn〕　　pretend〔prɪ'tɛnd〕
theater〔'θiətɚ〕

9

I often like to listen to the radio.

I like music that has a good dance beat!

I also like to practice singing.

I read magazines and comics.

Sometimes I read books, too.

Reading is fun and good for my mind!

These are the things I do in my free time.

I'm often busy with school and clubs.

When I have free time, I really enjoy it!

And that's the end of that. I'd like to thank you
for paying attention. See you around!

listen ('lɪsn̩)	*listen to*
radio ('redɪ,o)	music ('mjuzɪk)
dance (dæns)	beat (bit)
practice ('præktɪs)	sing (sɪŋ)
read (rid)	magazine (,mægə'zin)
book (bʊk)	mind (maɪnd)
busy ('bɪzɪ)	school (skul)
club (klʌb)	enjoy (ɪn'dʒɔɪ)

9

9. *What I Do in My Free Time*

● 演講解說

Wow! What a great-looking crowd! Would you like to know what I do in my free time?	哇！一大群人看起來好棒呀！你們想知道我在休閒時做什麼嗎？
We all get breaks from time to time. When I have free time, I rest. I rest by doing things that I like.	我們有時都有休息時間。當我有空閒時間，我就會休息。我休息時會做我喜歡做的事。
One of my hobbies is drawing. *I* like to draw characters from movies. *I* also draw animals and comics.	我其中一項嗜好是畫畫。我喜歡畫電影中的人物。我也喜歡畫動物跟漫畫。
Sometimes I play video games. This is fun to do alone or with friends. I don't play too much, though.	有時我會打電玩。自己打或是和朋友一起打電玩都很有趣。但是我不會玩得太過份。

9

** ——————————————

free〔fri〕*adj.* 自由的；空閒的　　*free time* 空閒時間
break〔brek〕*n.* 休息　　*from time to time* 有時；偶爾
rest〔rɛst〕*v.* 休息　　hobby〔'habɪ〕*n.* 嗜好　　draw〔drɔ〕*v.* 畫畫
character〔'kærɪktɚ〕*n.* 人物；角色　　movie〔'muvɪ〕*n.* 電影
animal〔'ænəml̩〕*n.* 動物　　comics〔'kamɪks〕*n. pl.* 漫畫
video〔'vɪdɪ,o〕*adj.* 電視的　　*video game* 電視遊戲
fun〔fʌn〕*adj.* 有趣的　　alone〔ə'lon〕*adv.* 獨自地
friend〔frɛnd〕*n.* 朋友　　though〔ðo〕*adv.* 然而

I like to talk to my friends on the Internet.

We write e-mails or chat.

We might also play online games together.

我喜歡跟朋友在網路上講話。

我們會寫電子郵件或聊天。

我們也可能會一起玩線上遊戲。

On sunny days, I play soccer and run fast.

When I play basketball, I try to jump high.

Playing sports with friends is fun!

晴天的時候，我會踢足球並快速奔跑。

當我打籃球時，我試著跳很高。

跟朋友一起運動很有趣！

On rainy days, or at night, I watch movies.

I like cartoons and action movies.

I eat popcorn and pretend I'm in a theater.

雨天的時候，或是晚上，我會看電影。

我喜歡卡通和動作片。

我會吃爆米花，並假裝自己在電影院裡。

**　*　*** ───────────────────

Internet〔'ɪntɚ͵nɛt〕*n.* 網路　　e-mail〔'i͵mel〕*n.* 電子郵件
chat〔tʃæt〕*v.* 聊天　　online〔͵ɑn'laɪn〕*adj.* 線上的
together〔tə'gɛðɚ〕*adv.* 一起　　sunny〔'sʌnɪ〕*adj.* 晴朗的
soccer〔'sɑkɚ〕*n.* 足球　　run〔rʌn〕*v.* 跑
fast〔fæst〕*adv.* 快速地　　basketball〔'bæskɪt͵bɔl〕*n.* 籃球
jump〔dʒʌmp〕*v.* 跳　　high〔haɪ〕*adv.* 高高地
sport〔sport〕*n.* 運動　　rainy〔'renɪ〕*adj.* 下雨的
night〔naɪt〕*n.* 夜晚　　cartoon〔kɑr'tun〕*n.* 卡通
action〔'ækʃən〕*n.* 動作　　*action movie* 動作片
popcorn〔'pɑp͵kɔrn〕*n.* 爆米花　　pretend〔prɪ'tɛnd〕*v.* 假裝
theater〔'θiətɚ〕*n.* 電影院

9

I often like to listen to the radio.

I like music that has a good
dance beat!

I also like to practice singing.

I read magazines and comics.

Sometimes I read books, too.

Reading is fun and good for my
mind!

These are the things I do in my
free time.

I'm often busy with school and clubs.

When I have free time, I really
enjoy it!

*And that's the end of that. I'd like to
thank you for paying attention.
See you around!*

我常常喜歡聽廣播。	
我喜歡有愉快的舞曲節奏的音樂！	
我也喜歡練習歌唱。	
我會看雜誌和漫畫。	
我有時也讀書。	
讀書很有趣，而且對我的心靈有幫助！	
這些就是我在空閒時會做的事。	
我常常忙於課堂和社團的事。	
當我有空時，我會真的很享受這些時光。	
我講完了。我想要謝謝你們注意聽我演講。待會兒見！	

9

** ─────────────────

listen〔'lɪsn̩〕*v.* 聽　　***listen to*** 聆聽
radio〔'redɪ‚o〕*n.* 廣播　　music〔'mjuzɪk〕*n.* 音樂
dance〔dæns〕*n.* 跳舞；舞曲　　beat〔bit〕*n.* 節奏；拍子
practice〔'præktɪs〕*v.* 練習　　sing〔sɪŋ〕*v.* 唱歌
read〔rid〕*v.* 閱讀　　magazine〔‚mægə'zin〕*n.* 雜誌
book〔bʊk〕*n.* 書　　mind〔maɪnd〕*n.* 心靈
busy〔'bɪzɪ〕*adj.* 忙碌的　　school〔skul〕*n.* 學校；學業
club〔klʌb〕*n.* 社團　　enjoy〔ɪn'dʒɔɪ〕*v.* 享受

● 背景說明

　　每天除了學校課業外，還有其他大大小小的事情，忙完以後，總算有了一些空閒時間，這時候你會做些什麼事呢？本篇演講稿，要教你如何善用空閒時間，培養其他的興趣或專長。

1. ***We all get breaks from time to time.***
   break〔brek〕*n.* 休息時間
   from time to time 有時候；偶爾

　　這句話的意思是「我們有時候會有休息時間。」break 在這裡是「休息時間」的意思，例如：

　　Let's take a ***break***.
　　（我們休息一下。）
　　I often take a nap during my lunch ***break***.
　　（午休時，我常會小睡一下。）

　　take a break 休息一下
　　nap〔næp〕*n.* 小睡　　***take a nap*** 小睡片刻
　　lunch break 午休

from time to time 就是「有時候；偶爾」(= *sometimes*) 的意思。例如：

　　From time to time, I like to go shopping.
　　（我偶爾喜歡去購物。）
　　shop〔ʃɑp〕*v.* 購物　　***go shopping*** 去購物

9

2. *One of my hobbies is drawing*.

hobby〔'hɑbɪ〕*n.* 嗜好　　draw〔drɔ〕*v.* 畫畫

　　這句話的意思是「我其中一項嗜好是畫畫。」本句使用：one of + 複數名詞 + 單數動詞，表示「…的其中之一」，one 也可以換成 some（一些）、most（大多）、all（所有）等，當然動詞要隨著單複數而改變型態：

One of the girls is going to get married.
（那些女孩中，其中一位要結婚了。）

Most of my classmates are boys.
（我的同學大多是男生。）

Neither of my parents smokes.
（我的雙親都不抽煙。）

marry〔'mɛrɪ〕*v.* 和…結婚　　*get married* 結婚
classmate〔'klæs,met〕*n.* 同班同學
neither〔'niðɚ〕*pron.* 兩者都不
smoke〔smok〕*v.* 抽煙

　　另外，hobby 是「嗜好」的意思，要小心不要寫成 habit（習慣），它們發音相近，但是意思不同：

What are your *hobbies*?
（你的嗜好是什麼？）

Old *habits* die hard.
（積習難改。）

old〔old〕*adj.* 長時間的　　habit〔'hæbɪt〕*n.* 習慣
die〔daɪ〕*v.* 停止；死亡
hard〔hɑrd〕*adv.* 困難地　　*die hard* 難戒除

3. *I don't play too much*, *though*.

though〔ðo〕*adv.* 然而

在本句中 though 是副詞，通常放在句中或句尾，意思是「然而」(= *however*)；though 放在句首時，是連接詞，作「雖然」解，等於 although。比較以下的句子：

Though (= *Although*) he is over 60, he still makes it a habit to exercise every day.
（雖然他已超過六十歲，仍每天保持運動的習慣。）

He still argued, *though* he knew he was wrong.（雖然他知道自己是錯的，他還是在爭辯。）

He can't study well; he sings well, *though*.
（他無法唸好書，然而他歌唱得很好）

I wish I could finish it, *though*.
（不過我希望我可以完成。）

habit〔'hæbɪt〕*n.* 習慣
make it a habit to + *V*. 習慣~
argue〔'ɑrgjʊ〕*v.* 爭論；辯駁　　wrong〔rɔŋ〕*adj.* 錯誤的
study〔'stʌdɪ〕*v.* 讀書　　sing〔sɪŋ〕*v.* 唱歌
wish〔wɪʃ〕*v.* 希望　　finish〔'fɪnɪʃ〕*v.* 完成

9

4. *When I play basketball*, *I try to jump high*.

basketball〔'bæskɪt,bɔl〕*n.* 籃球
play basketball 打籃球　　jump〔dʒʌmp〕*v.* 跳
high〔high〕*adv.* 高高地

play 常和活動做搭配，像是「運動」或「樂器」，此時要依照搭配來翻譯。如果是運動，不可以加冠詞：

I used to *play baseball* on weekends.
（我以前常在週末打棒球。）

I often go to the gym to *play badminton*.
（我常去體育館打羽毛球。）

play 若和樂器搭配，則要加定冠詞 the：

Learning to *play the guitar* is a challenge.
（學彈吉他是個挑戰。）

He has been *playing the violin* for
ten years.
（他已拉小提琴十年了。）

used to 以前　　baseball〔'bes,bɔl〕*n.* 棒球
weekend〔'wik'ɛnd〕*n.* 週末　　gym〔dʒɪm〕*n.* 體育館
badminton〔'bædmɪntən〕*n.* 羽毛球
guitar〔gɪ'tɑr〕*n.* 吉他
challenge〔'tʃælɪndʒ〕*n.* 挑戰
violin〔,vaɪə'lɪn〕*n.* 小提琴

high 可以當副詞，意思是「高高地」，要小心不要跟
highly 搞錯，意思是「非常」：

An eagle can fly *high* in the sky.
（老鷹可以在天空高飛。）

She is a *highly* educated woman.
（她是教育程度很高的女士。）

He is *highly* pleased. （他很高興。）

eagle〔'igl̩〕*n.* 老鷹
educated〔'ɛdʒu,ketɪd〕*adj.* 受教育的
pleased〔plizd〕*adj.* 高興的；滿意的

5. ***On rainy days*, *or at night*, *I watch movies*.**
   rainy〔ˊrenɪ〕*adj.* 下雨的
   movie〔ˊmuvɪ〕*n.* 電影

   「看電影」是 watch / see a movie，如果要說
   「去看電影」，則說成 go to a movie，例如：

   Do you want to ***see a movie*** tonight?
   （你今晚想看電影嗎？）

   Maybe we can ***go to a movie***.
   （或許我們可以去看個電影。）

   tonight〔 təˊnaɪt 〕*adv.* 今晚
   maybe〔ˊmebɪ〕*adv.* 或許；大概

   電影有很多種類，常見的有 horror movie（恐
   怖片）、action movie（動作片）、big-budget movie
   （大預算片）、hit movie（熱門片）：

   I like to see a ***horror movie*** at night.
   （我喜歡晚上看恐怖片。）

   Action movies always excite me.
   （動作片總是讓我熱血沸騰。）

   The ***big budget movie*** proved to be boring.
   （這大預算片結果是很無聊。）

   I go to see a ***hit movie*** every week.
   （我每週會去看一部熱門電影。）

   excite〔 ɪkˊsaɪt 〕*v.* 使興奮
   prove〔 pruv 〕*v.*（結果）成為
   boring〔ˊborɪŋ〕*adj.* 無聊的

9

6. ***I also like to practice singing.***
practice〔'præktɪs〕*v. n.* 練習
sing〔sɪŋ〕*v.* 唱歌

　　practice（練習）的後面須接動名詞或名詞；
practice 也可當名詞。

　　My brother ***practices dancing*** every day.
　　（我弟弟每天練習跳舞。）

　　Practice makes perfect.（熟能生巧。）

dance〔dæns〕*v.* 跳舞
perfect〔'pɝfɪkt〕*adj.* 完美的

7. ***I am often busy with school and clubs.***
busy〔'bɪzɪ〕*adj.* 忙碌　　***be busy with*** 忙於
school〔skul〕*n.* 學校；課業　　club〔klʌb〕*n.* 社團

　　busy 的用法要注意，可以是 be busy with + N，
或是 be busy + (in) + V-ing：

　　Most students ***are busy with*** schoolwork.
　　（大多學生都忙於課業。）

　　My boss ***is*** now ***busy with*** a customer.
　　（我老闆現正忙於處理客戶。）

　　He ***is*** now ***busy studying*** for exams.
　　（他正忙於讀書準備考試。）

schoolwork〔'skul,wɝk〕*n.* 課業
customer〔'kʌstəmɚ〕*n.* 顧客
exam〔ɪg'zæm〕*n.* 考試（= *examination*）

○ 作文範例

What I Do in My Free Time

People like to do different things in their free time. When I have free time, I do things that I like. One of my hobbies is drawing. I like to draw animals and comics. *Sometimes* I play computer games. I play them with friends or alone. I *also* use the Internet to write emails or chat with my friends. On sunny days, I play soccer or basketball. Playing sports with friends is fun! On rainy days, I like to watch movies or listen to music. I *also* like to read magazines and comics. These are the things I do in my free time. *Most of the time*, I am busy with school. *So* when I have free time, I really enjoy it.

9

● 中文翻譯

我在空閒時會做的事

　　人們在空閒時喜歡做不同的事情。當我有空閒時，我會做我喜歡的事情。我其中一個興趣是畫畫。我喜歡畫動物和漫畫。有時候我打電玩。我會跟朋友打或是自己打電玩。我也會用網路寫電子郵件或是和朋友聊天。晴天的時候，我會踢足球或打籃球。和朋友一起運動很有趣！雨天的時候，我喜歡看電影或聽音樂。我也喜歡看雜誌和漫畫。這些是我空閒時會做的事。大多時候，我忙於課業。所以當我有空閒時，我會真的很享受這些時光。

10. What Makes Me Happy

Dear friends. It's an honor to be here today.
Would you like to know what makes me happy?

Life is suffering.
A respected man once said this.
Life can be happy too, though.

Like everyone else, I like to be happy.
Certain things bring me happiness.
I will tell you about what makes me happy.

I like to have holidays with my family.
We share a lot of fun times and love.
That is a very good experience.

happy (ˈhæpɪ)
suffering (ˈsʌfərɪŋ)
once (wʌns)
like (laɪk)
certain (ˈsɝtn̩)
happiness (ˈhæpɪnɪs)
family (ˈfæməlɪ)
fun (fʌn)
love (lʌv)

life (laɪf)
respected (rɪˈspɛktɪd)
though (ðo)
else (ˈɛls)
bring (brɪŋ)
holiday (ˈhɑləˌde)
share (ʃɛr)
time (taɪm)
experience (ɪkˈspɪrɪəns)

10

Being in nature makes me happy.

I like to look at flowers and plants.

Watching animals and birds is nice, too.

I enjoy eating good food.

It's nice to take time to eat well.

It improves my body and my mood.

Being with my friends makes
  me happy.

We laugh and play together.

I smile a lot and feel loved.

10

nature〔'netʃɚ 〕   flower〔'flauɚ 〕

plant〔 plænt 〕   watch〔 watʃ 〕

animal〔'ænəml̩ 〕   bird〔 bɝd 〕

nice〔 naɪs 〕   enjoy〔 ɪn'dʒɔɪ 〕

take〔 tek 〕   improve〔 ɪm'pruv 〕

body〔'badɪ 〕   mood〔 mud 〕

friend〔 frɛnd 〕   laugh〔 læf 〕

together〔 tə'gɛðɚ 〕   smile〔 smaɪl 〕

feel〔 fil 〕

I like cold water on hot days.

Warm blankets on cold days are great.

Big hugs when I'm sad make me happy.

Some people think they need a lot.

I don't need expensive things to be happy.

I don't need fancy things to be happy.

Simple things make life sweet.

Most good things can't be seen or held.

Life's joys are many, and all around us!

So that's what makes me happy. I really hope you agree. Thanks for listening and have a great day!

---

cold ﹝ kold ﹞

hot ﹝ hɑt ﹞

blanket ﹝'blæŋkɪt ﹞

hug ﹝ hʌg ﹞

need ﹝ nid ﹞

expensive ﹝ ɪk'spɛnsɪv ﹞

simple ﹝'sɪmpḷ ﹞

held ﹝ hɛld ﹞

around ﹝ ə'raʊnd ﹞

water ﹝'wɔtɚ ﹞

warm ﹝ wɔrm ﹞

great ﹝ gret ﹞

sad ﹝ sæd ﹞

a lot

fancy ﹝'fænsɪ ﹞

sweet ﹝ swit ﹞

joy ﹝ dʒɔɪ ﹞

10

10. *What Makes Me Happy*

● 演講解說

Dear friends. It's an honor to be here today. Would you like to know what makes me happy?	親愛的朋友。今天很榮幸來到這裡。你想要聽聽什麼讓我感到快樂嗎？
Life is suffering. *A respected man once said this.* *Life can be happy too, though.*	人生是場苦難。 一位受人尊敬的人曾這麼說過。 但是人生可以是快樂的。
Like everyone else, I like to be happy. Certain things bring me happiness. I will tell you about what makes me happy.	就像其他人，我喜歡快樂。 某些事物能帶給我快樂。 我來告訴你什麼會使我開心。
I like to have holidays with my family. We share a lot of fun times and love. That is a very good experience.	我喜歡和家人度過假日。 我們會一起分享有趣的時光和愛。 那是非常美好的經驗。

** ————

happy〔'hæpɪ〕*adj.* 快樂的　　life〔laɪf〕*n.* 人生；生命
suffering〔'sʌfərɪŋ〕*n.* 苦難；痛苦
respected〔rɪ'spɛktɪd〕*adj.* 受尊敬的　　once〔wʌns〕*adv.* 曾經
though〔ðo〕*adv.* 然而　　like〔laɪk〕*prep.* 像
else〔ɛls〕*adj.* 其他的　　certain〔'sɝtn̩〕*adj.* 某些
bring〔brɪŋ〕*v.* 帶給　　happiness〔'hæpɪnɪs〕*n.* 快樂；幸福
holiday〔'hɑlə,de〕*n.* 假日　　family〔'fæməlɪ〕*n.* 家人
share〔ʃɛr〕*v.* 分享　　fun〔fʌn〕*adj.* 有趣的
time〔taɪm〕*n.* 時光；一段期間　　love〔lʌv〕*n.* 愛
experience〔ɪk'spɪrɪəns〕*n.* 經驗

10

Being in nature makes me happy. 　置身於大自然會讓我開心。

I like to look at flowers and plants. 　我喜歡看花和植物。

Watching animals and birds is
　　nice, too. 　看動物和鳥也很好。

I enjoy eating good food. 　我喜歡吃美食。

It's nice to take time to eat well. 　能花時間好好吃飯很不錯。

It improves my body and my
　　mood. 　這能改善我的身體和心情。

Being with my friends makes me
　　happy. 　和朋友在一起讓我感到快樂。

We laugh and play together. 　我們會一起笑，而且一起玩。

I smile a lot and feel loved. 　我常常笑，而且能感受到愛。

※※

nature〔ˈnetʃɚ〕*n.* 大自然　　*look at* 看　　flower〔ˈflauɚ〕*n.* 花

plant〔plænt〕*n.* 植物　　watch〔watʃ〕*v.* 看

animal〔ˈænəml̩〕*n.* 動物　　bird〔bɜd〕*n.* 鳥

enjoy〔ɪnˈdʒɔɪ〕*v.* 喜歡；享受　　take〔tek〕*v.* 花（時間）

improve〔ɪmˈpruv〕*v.* 改善；增進

body〔ˈbadɪ〕*n.* 身體　　mood〔mud〕*n.* 心情

friend〔frɛnd〕*n.* 朋友　　laugh〔læf〕*v.* 笑

together〔təˈgɛðɚ〕*adv.* 一起

smile〔smaɪl〕*v.* 微笑　　*a lot* 常常

10

I like cold water on hot days.	天氣熱時，我喜歡冷水。
Warm blankets on cold days are great.	天氣冷時，溫暖的毯子很棒。
Big hugs when I'm sad make me happy.	難過時，大大的擁抱能讓我高興。
Some people think they need a lot.	有些人認為他們需要很多東西。
I don't need expensive things to be happy.	我並不需要昂貴的東西才會開心。
I don't need fancy things to be happy.	我不需要酷炫的東西才會快樂。
Simple things make life sweet.	簡單的事物讓生命甜美。
Most good things can't be seen or held.	大多美好的事物是看不見或握不住的。
Life's joys are many, and all around us!	生命的快樂有很多，而且就在我們的周圍！
So that's what makes me happy. *I really hope you agree. Thanks for listening and have a great day!*	那就是讓我快樂的事物。我真的希望你們也有同感。謝謝你們聽我演講，祝你們有個美好的一天！

**

cold〔kold〕*adj.* 冷的　　water〔'wɔtɚ〕*n.* 水
hot〔hɑt〕*adj.* 熱的　　warm〔wɔrm〕*adj.* 溫暖的
blanket〔'blæŋkɪt〕*n.* 毯子　　great〔gret〕*adj.* 很棒的
hug〔hʌg〕*n.* 擁抱　　sad〔sæd〕*adj.* 難過的　　need〔nid〕*v.* 需要
a lot 大量；很多　　expensive〔ɪk'spɛnsɪv〕*adj.* 昂貴的
fancy〔'fænsɪ〕*adj.* 酷炫的；昂貴的
simple〔'sɪmpḷ〕*adj.* 簡單的　　sweet〔swit〕*adj.* 甜美的
held〔hɛld〕*v.* 握住（hold 的過去式和過去分詞）
joy〔dʒɔɪ〕*n.* 快樂　　around〔ə'raʊnd〕*prep.* 在…周圍

10

● 背景說明

　　　本篇演講稿主要是要描述讓自己快樂的事物，要獲得快樂的方法很多，有些人以奢侈的生活為樂，有些人則偏好樸實無華的生活方式，各有所好。看看你要如何描述讓你感到快樂的生活。

1. ***Life is suffering.***
   life〔laɪf〕*n.* 人生；生命
   suffering〔'sʌfərɪŋ〕*n.* 苦難；受苦

　　　這句話的意思是「人生是場苦難。」意思就是：Life is full of suffering. 或是 Life is filled with suffering. (生命充滿著苦難。) 佛教認為，生命之所以有苦難，是因為人的慾望，若要超脫，唯一之道就是控制慾望：

　　Life is filled with suffering from birth to
　　　　death. (生命自始至終都充滿苦難。)

　　Suffering is caused by people wanting
　　　　earthly things.
　　(苦難是因為人們想要世俗的事物所造成。)

　　By controlling wants, suffering will end.
　　(藉由控制需求，苦難便會停止。)

be full of 充滿 (= *be filled with*)
birth〔bɝθ〕*n.* 出生　　death〔dɛθ〕*n.* 死亡
from birth to death 從生到死；自始至終
cause〔kɔz〕*v.* 造成　　earthly〔'ɝθlɪ〕*adj.* 世俗的
control〔kən'trol〕*v.* 控制　wants〔wɑnts〕*n. pl.* 需求
end〔ɛnd〕*v.* 結束

10

2. *A respected man once said this*.

respected〔rɪ'spɛktɪd〕*adj.* 受尊敬的
once〔wʌns〕*adv.* 曾經

respect 動詞和名詞一樣，是「尊敬」的意思，
因為人是「受到尊敬的」，所以用 respected（受尊敬
的），respect 還有其他三個形容詞：respectable
（值得尊敬的）、respectful（恭敬的）、respective
（各自的），要注意它們的差別：

Respect others if you would have others
respect you.
（要他人尊敬你，你得先尊敬他人。）

Professor Wang is a **respectable** scholar.
（王教授是值得尊敬的學者。）

He is **respectful** to his elders.
（他對長輩很恭敬。）

All men have their **respective** duties.
（每個人都有各自的責任。）

respect〔rɪ'spɛkt〕*n. v.* 尊敬
respectable〔rɪ'spɛktəbḷ〕*adj.* 值得尊敬的
respectful〔rɪ'spɛktfəl〕*adj.* 恭敬的
respective〔rɪ'spɛktɪv〕*adj.* 各自的
professor〔prə'fɛsɚ〕*n.* 教授
scholar〔'skɑlɚ〕*n.* 學者
elders〔'ɛldɚz〕*n. pl.* 長輩
duty〔'djutɪ〕*n.* 責任；職責

10

3. *Certain things bring me happiness*.

certain〔ˋsɝtn̩〕*adj.* 某些　　bring〔brɪŋ〕*v.* 帶給
happiness〔ˋhæpɪnɪs〕*n.* 快樂；幸福

這句話的意思是「某些事物能帶給我快樂。」certain
在此是作「某些」(= *some*) 解，不是「確定的」(= *sure*)
的意思，要依上下文來判斷：

I am *certain* I will pass the exam.
（我確定我會通過考試。）

It's not *certain* where he will go.
（無法確定他會去哪裡。）

I agree with you to a *certain* extent.
（在某個程度上我同意你。）

An organism lives in a *certain* place to
meet its needs.
（生物需要活在某個地方，才能滿足它的需求。）

It takes a *certain* amount of effort to
reach the goal.
（需要一些努力才能達到目標。）

pass〔pæs〕*v.* 通過　　exam〔ɪgˋzæm〕*n.* 考試
agree〔əˋgri〕*v.* 同意　　*agree with* 同意
extent〔ɪkˋstɛnt〕*n.* 程度
to a…extent 就…的程度
organism〔ˋɔrgənͺɪzəm〕*n.* 生物；有機體
meet〔mit〕*v.* 滿足　　needs〔nidz〕*n. pl.* 需求
take〔tek〕*v.* 需要　　amount〔əˋmaʊnt〕*n.* 量
effort〔ˋɛfət〕*n.* 努力　　reach〔ritʃ〕*v.* 達到
goal〔gol〕*n.* 目標

10

4. *I will tell you about what makes me happy.*

　　這句話的意思是「我來告訴你什麼會讓我開心。」what 引導名詞子句，為子句中的主詞，等於 the thing that (*or* which)，也可以是名詞子句中的受詞或補語：

　　Tell me *what*'s on your mind.【主詞】
　　（告訴我你在想什麼。）

　　I don't know *what* you want.【受詞】
　　（我不知道你要什麼。）

　　Let's see *what* the fuss is about.【主詞補語】
　　（我們來看看有什麼好大驚小怪的。）

　　mind〔maɪnd〕*n.* 心智；思想
　　on one's mind 思考；想
　　fuss〔fʌs〕*n.* 忙亂；大驚小怪
　　what the fuss is about 發生什麼事；有什麼好大驚小怪的

5. *Being in nature makes me happy.*
　　nature〔'netʃɚ〕*n.* 大自然；自然界
　　happy〔'hæpɪ〕*adj.* 快樂的

　　這句話的意思是「置身於大自然讓我感到開心。」Being in nature 是動名詞當主詞，要注意 nature 不要隨意加冠詞，若寫成 the nature，則是指「本質；天性」。

　　What is *the nature* of your work?
　　（你工作的性質是什麼？）

　　work〔wɝk〕*n.* 工作

10

6. *It's nice to take time to eat well.*

take〔tek〕*v.* 花（時間）

這句話的意思是「能花時間好好地吃飯是很好的。」
take time + to V. 的意思是「騰出時間做某事」，
例如：

While in Taipei he *took time* to visit
　his friends.
（在台北的時候，他挪出時間拜訪朋友。）

I *take time* to read every day.
（我每天都騰出時間閱讀。）

visit〔'vɪzɪt〕*v.* 拜訪　　read〔rid〕*v.* 閱讀

take time 若以「事物」作為主詞，則是「需要…時間」：

Love *takes time*.（愛需要時間。）

Being an expert *takes time*.（成為專家需要時間。）

【expert〔'ɛkspət〕*n.* 專家】

另外，take *one's* time + V-ing 是「慢慢地做某事」：

There is no hurry.　You may *take your time*.
（不急，你可以慢慢來。）

I *took my time* taking a shower.
（我慢條斯理地淋浴。）

hurry〔'hɝɪ〕*n.* 匆忙
shower〔'ʃauə〕*n.* 淋浴　　*take a shower* 淋浴

10

7. *Some people think they need a lot.*

need〔nid〕*v.* 需要　　***a lot*** 很多；大量

這句話的意思是「有些人覺得他們需要很多事物。」
a lot 在這是名詞，表示「很多；大量」，也可寫成 lots：

Parents have to spend *a lot* on children's
education.（父母必須花費許多在孩子的教育上。）

I still have *a lot* to learn.（我仍有許多要學習。）

It's a big country, with *lots* to see and do.
（這是個很大的國家，有很多東西可看可做。）

have to 必須　　children〔'tʃɪldrən〕*n. pl.* 兒童（child 的複數）
education〔‚ɛdjʊ'keʃən〕*n.* 教育　　still〔stɪl〕*adv.* 仍然
country〔'kaʊntrɪ〕*n.* 國家

8. *Simple things make life sweet.*

simple〔'sɪmpl̩〕*adj.* 樸實的；簡單的
sweet〔swit〕*adj.* 甜美的

這句的意思是「簡單的事物讓生命甜美。」也就是
說，生活簡單，就可以過得快樂，許多名人都有類似
的想法：

Life is very simple, but we insist on making it
complicated.（生命很簡單，但我們堅持把它變複
雜；世上本無事，庸人自擾之。）

Who is rich?　He who rejoices in his portion.
（誰最富有？能自得其樂的人。）

insist〔ɪn'sɪst〕*v.* 堅持　　***insist on + V-ing / N*** 堅持～
complicated〔'kɑmplə‚ketɪd〕*adj.* 複雜的
rich〔rɪtʃ〕*adj.* 有錢的；富有的
rejoice〔rɪ'dʒɔɪs〕*v.* 高興　　portion〔'porʃən〕*n.* 命運

● 作文範例

What Makes Me Happy

Like everyone else, I like to be happy. Certain things make me happy. *First*, I like to have holidays with my family. We share a lot of fun times and love. Being in nature *also* makes me happy. I like to look at flowers and watch animals. *Third*, I enjoy eating good food. It is good for my health and my mood. Being with my friends makes me happy, too. We like to laugh and play together. I like cold water on hot days, warm blankets on cold days, and big hugs any time. Some people think they need a lot of things. *But* I don't need things to be happy. Most good things can't be seen or held. Happiness is all around us.

10

● 中文翻譯

令我快樂的事物

　　就像其他人一樣，我喜歡快樂。某些事物能帶給我快樂。第一，我喜歡和我的家人度過假日。我會一起分享有趣的時光和愛。置身於大自然也會讓我快樂。我喜歡看花和動物。第三，我喜歡吃美食。這對我的健康和心情有幫助。和朋友在一起也讓我感到快樂。我們喜歡一起笑，而且一起玩。天氣熱時，我喜歡冷水，天氣冷時，我喜歡溫暖的毯子，在任何時候，我喜歡大大的擁抱。有些人認為他們需要很多東西。但我不需要有東西才會快樂。大多美好的事物是看不見或握不住的。快樂就在我們的周圍。

10

這10篇演講稿，
你都背下來了嗎？
現在請利用下面的提示，
不斷地複習。

以下你可以看到每篇演講稿的格式，
三句為一組，九句為一段，每篇演講稿共
三段，27句，看起來是不是輕鬆好背呢？
不要猶豫，趕快開始背了！每篇
演講稿只要能背到1分半鐘內，
就終生不忘！

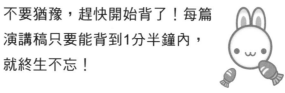

1. My Favorite Animal

There are many nice animals ….
My favorite animal is the dog.
Dogs are smart, kind animals.

The first dog I saw was at a ….
He was a little white puppy.
He played with me and did tricks.

After that, I loved all dogs.
Every time I hear a dog bark, ….
I like to read books about dogs, too.

Sometimes I wish I could have ….
I asked my parents, but they said no.
Soon, they might change their minds.

Until then, I help friends with ….
I feed the neighbor's puppy ….
He jumps and licks my face.

Dogs have many talents.
They can find lost people.
They can swim well.

Dogs can also protect their families.
They bark when any danger ….
These dogs are animal heroes.

Some dogs are not nice or safe.
They make scary noises and ….
I stay away from those dogs!

Most dogs and puppies are nice.
If I get a dog, I will love him!
I want all people to like dogs, too.

2. My Favorite Story

I like to listen to stories.
Stories can be sad, happy, or scary.
My favorite one is "The Three ….

I will tell you the story now.
A long time ago, there were three pigs.
They lived with their mother ….

One day, they left home to be on ….
The first little pig was lazy.
He did not like hard work.

Because of this, he did ….
He built his house from straw.
The second pig was also lazy.

He built his house from thin wood.
The third pig was smart and not lazy.
He built his house with rocks.

The third pig's house was very strong.
All three pigs were happy for a while.
Then, a big bad wolf came to ….

He blew down the first pig's house.
The pig ran to his brother's house.
The wolf blew down the second ….

The pigs ran to their smart ….
The wolf tried to blow down ….
The rock house was too strong to fall!

Safe inside, they laughed at the wolf.
The wolf was angry and left ….
The pig brothers were very happy.

3. If I Were Superman

It doesn't matter if you're a boy ....
You have to agree, Superman is cool.
Everyone admires him!

I sometimes pretend to be Superman.
I think about all the things I could do.
My powers would be amazing!

I'd leap tall buildings in a ....
People would call me a hero!
There would be a serious side ....

Superman knows what a real hero is.
A real hero is responsible and giving.
That's why Superman helps people.

If I were Superman, I'd help ....
I would stop the bad guys.
I would fight crime and save lives.

Sometimes I would have breaks, ...
During those times, I would have fun!
Nothing would be too hard for me.

Sports would be no problem.
I would be so strong and fast!
In no time I could be a famous athlete.

I would fly through the sky fast!
I could travel around the world ....
I would be invited to many parties!

These are some of the things ....
It's fun to imagine being Superman.
But, I am happy being myself, too.

4. An Unforgettable Trip

One day, my family took a trip.
We went to a nearby town ....
It began as a nice, sunny day.

As we shopped, the sky ....
For lunch, we went to a restaurant.
We sat at our table and looked outside.

Through a window, we could see ....
It was filled with dark, angry clouds.
It was about to storm outside!

The storm started as our meal ....
The waiter was nervous ....
We heard the cooks talk about it.

Everyone was very scared.
The wind blew hard and ....
We saw trees being blown over.

Garbage and dust blew past ....
We tried to eat our lunch.
There was nothing else we could do!

At last the storm ended.
We left the restaurant to shop more.
The town was a mess from the storm.

In the evening, we returned home.
I couldn't forget the storm.
It was exciting and scary ....

I had though going shopping ....
I didn't even want to go.
Instead, it became an ....

5. An Important Lesson

I learned a very important lesson ….
It was a hard lesson to learn.
I will tell you about it, *now*.

I had a cute little dog.
He was my best friend ….
It was my job to take care of him.

Sometimes I'd get lazy ….
I didn't always take good care ….
I would neglect him sometimes.

I didn't comb his fur often, *though*.
He didn't get bathed enough, either.
Sometimes I wouldn't take him ….

My dog stayed in a cage by our house.
Dad told me to always do one thing.
He told me to always lock the gate ….

The lock was hard to close sometimes.
If I was in a hurry, I didn't do it.
One day, the gate came open.

My dog escaped and ran ….
I was very scared as I searched ….
What if something bad happened ….

We found him, but he had a hurt leg.
We bandaged it, but he was in pain.
I felt very sad about it.

I learned that I needed to be ….
I need to do things the right way ….
I took good care of my dog after that!

6. A Scary Experience

Have you ever been afraid ….
I was once in total darkness.
It was really a scary experience.

It happened during a typhoon.
The winds outside were blowing ….
The rain was coming down hard.

I was sitting at home with my family.
Mom called us over for dinner.
We made our way over to the kitchen.

Suddenly, *the lights went out!*
We all sat quietly for a while.
I didn't know what to do!

I couldn't see anything at all.
The television wasn't working.
My computer wouldn't turn on.

I looked outside the window.
It was completely dark outside.
There weren't any lights at all.

I started to panic!
What if there were ghosts?
What if there were monsters?

Just then, the lights came back on.
I could see my family again.
I was so relieved!

The typhoon had caused a blackout.
It was very scary at the time.
I was glad it didn't last very long!

7. Going to the Night Market

Sometimes I go to the night market.
Usually, I go with my parents.
It is fun and exciting!

At night, the marketplace is lit up.
The lights are any color ….
It is a beautiful sight.

There are many people, and it's noisy.
Vendors shout, and loud music ….
Everyone is moving and busy.

My parents take me to food stands.
I buy little snacks, and try ….
Sometimes we eat at a restaurant.

I always play at least one carnival ….
I like it when I win a prize!
I get better at the games each time ….

Tourists go to our night market.
I often see them there, taking photos.
They come from all over the world!

If I find something I like, I buy it.
Last weekend I bought a shirt there.
I also buy music and toys sometimes.

My friends meet me at ….
We go off together to look around.
Later, we rejoin our parents ….

The night market is a great place ….
There are many fun things to do there.
You should visit it, too!

8. How I Spend My Money

Money can be a wonderful tool.
You can use it to buy things you need.
Sometimes, money buys things ….

I don't have much money.
When I do have it, I spend it ….
My parents buy stuff that I need, ….

I buy new computer games.
My friend and I get the same games.
That way, we can play them together!

Sometimes, I buy action figures.
They are based on movie characters.
Some are modeled after ….

I might use my money to buy candy.
I use my money to play games ….
My friends and I have a good time!

Once, I saved my money to buy ….
I wanted a new, fancy one.
I was excited when I finally bought it!

I buy hats or shoes that I like.
Or I might buy a new school bag.
I want to look cool.

If there's nothing I want, I save ….
I can spend it if I go to ….
Or I can use it to buy a gift ….

Having money is nice.
Sometimes I spend it; sometimes ….
I always end up spending it ….

9. What I Do in My Free Time

We all get breaks from time to time.
When I have free time, I rest.
I rest by doing things that I like.

One of my hobbies is drawing.
I like to draw characters from movies.
I also draw animals and comics.

Sometimes I play video games.
This is fun to do alone or with friends.
I don't play too much, though.

I like to talk to my friends ….
We write e-mails or chat.
We might also play online games ….

On sunny days, I play soccer ….
When I play basketball, I try to ….
Playing sports with friends is fun!

On rainy days, or at night, I ….
I like cartoons and action movies.
I eat popcorn and pretend I'm in ….

I often like to listen to the radio.
I like music that has a good dance ….
I also like to practice singing.

I read magazines and comics.
Sometimes I read books, too.
Reading is fun and good for my mind!

These are the things I do in my ….
I'm often busy with school and clubs.
When I have free time, I really ….

10. What Makes Me Happy

Life is suffering.
A respected man once said this.
Life can be happy too, though.

Like everyone else, I like to be happy.
Certain things bring me happiness.
I will tell you about what makes ….

I like to have holidays with my family.
We share a lot of fun times and love.
That is a very good experience.

Being in nature makes me happy.
I like to look at flowers and plants.
Watching animals and birds is nice ….

I enjoy eating good food.
It's nice to take time to eat well.
It improves my body and my mood.

Being with my friends makes ….
We laugh and play together.
I smile a lot and feel loved.

I like cold water on hot days.
Warm blankets on cold days are great.
Big hugs when I'm sad make me ….

Some people think they need a lot.
I don't need expensive things to ….
I don't need fancy things to be happy.

Simple things make life sweet.
Most good things can't be seen ….
Life's joys are many, and all ….

「一口氣背少兒英語演講①」背誦記錄表

篇　　　　　　　　　名	口試通過日期	口試老師簽名
1. My Favorite Animal	年　　月　　日	
2. My Favorite Story	年　　月　　日	
3. If I Were Superman	年　　月　　日	
4. An Unforgettable Trip	年　　月　　日	
5. An Important Lesson	年　　月　　日	
6. A Scary Experience	年　　月　　日	
7. Going to the Night Market	年　　月　　日	
8. How I Spend My Money	年　　月　　日	
9. What I Do in My Free Time	年　　月　　日	
10. What Makes Me Happy	年　　月　　日	
全部 10 篇演講總複試	年　　月　　日	

　　自己背演講，很難專心，背給別人聽，是最有效的方法。練習的程序是：自己背 ➡ 背給同學聽 ➡ 背給老師聽 ➡ 在全班面前發表演講。可在教室裡、任何表演舞台或台階上，二、三個同學一組練習，比賽看誰背得好，效果甚佳。

　　天天聽著 CD，模仿美國人的發音和語調，英文自然就越說越溜。英語演講背多後，隨時都可以滔滔不絕，口若懸河。